Waiting for Love's Return

(Second Chances Series #5)

by
Morris Fenris

Waiting for Love's Return

Copyright 2017 by Morris Fenris,

Changing Culture Publications

Table of Contents

Prologue

Colorado Springs, Colorado, Four months earlier, mid-June...

Major Jeff Young was no longer enjoying his time as a newbie trainer. He and his Special Forces team were currently waiting for their next mission orders, and while they recuperated from the last horrible mission in the jungles of South America, they'd been pressed into service helping to train the new recruits on the mock battlefield.

Currently, the two dozen young men, some of them looking more like pre-teens than adult men, were navigating the obstacle course that had plagued so many that had come before them. Blank mortar fire, fog, the sound of machine gun fire, and small explosions created a measure of reality, and the young men were supposed to beat their previous time. They had been training on this course for the last four weeks, and today's exercise was the last time they would do so in the daylight. Starting a few days from now, they would be expected to navigate the same course in the dead of night and Jeff could already tell that more than a few of them were going to fail.

The young man he was currently watching had the slowest time of his group, and Jeff wondered what could have possessed a kid like that to enlist in the military. He was small in stature, and each time the machine guns fired, he flinched. The fact that Jeff could tell that from his observation post twenty yards away was not a good sign. The kid finally made it over the rope wall and headed for the ditches with the barbwire strung twelve inches above the ground.

The kid sloshed through the mud and dove for the lowest spot he could find, and Jeff felt like cursing when he realized the kid had forgotten to remove his pack. He knew their regular instructors would have gone over this time and again, but wearing their packs during this part of the exercise was just plain stupid. The barbed wire didn't allow for any extra clearance and almost immediately, the kid's pack became snared by the barbs.

"We've got a problem...," began Derek Evans, Jeff's teammate and best friend.

"Yeah, I see him. That kid should have stayed home and gone to college. He's not cut out for this stuff." Jeff grabbed a pair of wire cutters from the wall behind him and prepared to go rescue the kid who was starting to panic.

"Be careful," Derek warned him.

Jeff grinned, "I always am."

"Debatable," Derek shot back with a grin of his own. "Want me to send the rest of them off to clean up?"

"Please! Don't keep them around on his account. Let their regular instructors deal with them for the rest of the afternoon."

"Will do. You up for some pool later?" Derek asked, turning his attention back to the rest of the newbies finishing the course.

"Maybe. If not, I'll see you back at the barracks later." Jeff ducked out of the blind, wire cutters in hand and started barking orders to the young man who was now struggling to free himself and making matters even worse.

"Freeze! Don't move another muscle until I get your pack out of those wires. How many times have you been instructed to remove your packs before going under the wire? Were you listening at all, soldier?"

Jeff reached the kid and once again couldn't get over how young he looked. "Hold still."

The kid, hearing his voice, panicked and did the exact opposite. "Sir, I can get out of this. Maybe if I got backwards..."

"Did you hear my words, soldier, or are your ears full of mud?!"

"I heard you sir, but I really want to finish this on my own…"

"Then you should listen to instructions and remove your pack before attempting this part of the course." Jeff was straddling the kid's hips and reached down to cut the first wire, hoping there wasn't too much tension on the wire and it wouldn't snap back. The kid's pack was impossibly tangled in the wires from his struggles, and there wasn't any other way to get him out from under the wires without risking him getting sliced up by the barbs on the wire.

Jeff snipped the first wire and breathed a sigh of relief when nothing bounced back at him. He used his hands to bend the wire out of the way and was just reaching for the second wire, when the kid did what he'd been told not to. He moved. He'd evidently felt the pressure on his pack release and attempted to scoot himself backwards, but Jeff's arms were already just above the intact wires and the movement sent them rising up, the barbs digging into the soft flesh of his underarm.

Jeff clenched his jaw, not giving into the need to curse like so many of his other teammates would have done by now. He saw no reason to use vulgar language to express himself, and this time was no different. He took a shallow breath, forcing the sting of the injury away, and bit out, "Hold! Still!"

"Sorry, sir. I'm sorry, did you get cut…"

"Just hold still. Don't talk. Don't even breathe for the next thirty seconds." Jeff moved his arm away, feeling the wet warmth of his own blood dripping down his arm and he finished cutting the last wire. Once it was bent away from the pack, Jeff undid the buckles on the strap and lifted the pack with his good arm, "Get yourself out from under these wires."

The kid wasted no time in complying and before Jeff could walk his way out of the wires, the kid was standing in the mud, looking dejected and fearful. Jeff could have read him the riot act, but the throbbing pain in his arm, and the fact that the kid was obviously very contrite for having caused the situation= was enough for him.

Jeff handed him his pack, "Get out of here and don't forget to remove your pack next time."

"Yes, sir." The kid grabbed the pack and then pulled himself up straight, offering Jeff a salute. Jeff waved him off, and then turned and headed for the beginning of the course.

He glanced at his arm and sighed when he realized there was no way a couple of butterfly strips and antibiotic gel were going to fix this. He needed stitches and that meant a trip to the base hospital. *Not how I wanted to spend the rest of the afternoon at all. I hate training the newbies!*

He grabbed a towel from the bag he'd left at the training office, and then headed for the front of the building. He grabbed the first empty Jeep and drove himself over to the hospital, resigning himself to the process he knew was to come.

The hospital was busy and he was shuffled off to a waiting room, given a fresh bandage to press against the wound, and promised that someone would be in to see him shortly. He used the sink in the room to wash his hands and rinse the wounds out as best as he could, gritting his teeth as he applied pressure to the wound so that a fresh supply of blood would help clean any remaining debris from the punctures.

"You know I'm still going to have to clean it, right?" a bright voice asked from behind him.

Jeff looked over his shoulder and couldn't help but stare at the beautiful young woman standing there. She had red hair with a mixture of golden orange and burgundy streaks running through it, and her eyes reminded him of grass in the springtime. Realizing he was staring at her, he shut off the water and grabbed a fresh towel to cover the wounds, "I think I did a pretty good job."

She nodded and then walked towards him, "Why don't you let me be the judge of that? Hop up on the table and I'll be right there." She took his place at the sink, lathering her hands up and drying them before donning a pair of gloves.

Jeff couldn't get over how attracted he was to this young woman. Her voice was soft, but not weak, and there was a faint Southern drawl to some of her letters. "You're not from around here."

She smiled at him, pulling over a tray filled with supplies, "No, I'm from Georgia."

Jeff's raised a brow and commented, "That's a long way from Colorado. What brought you here?"

"I signed up to be a travelling nurse. I got a position here, but since I've worked with kids before, they offered me a permanent position and bought out my contract." She smiled at him and then frowned, "I'm afraid this is going to sting quite a bit."

Jeff nodded and clenched the end of the table with his good hand, "I'll handle it." He watched as she set a metal tray beneath his arm and then poured a liberal amount of Betadine over the wound. She was right; it did sting like he'd landed in a bed of nettles, but then she was washing the sting away with some sterile water and he took a shallow breath, releasing the pain from before.

"You still doing okay?" she asked with concern in her voice.

"I'm doing fine."

"So, how did this happen?" she asked as she probed the wounds, making sure they were cleaned out and ready to be stitched up.

"Training accident. They going to need stitches?" he asked her.

"Yes. Let me get the doctor on call. It shouldn't be too much longer now." She moved the tray of medical supplies away from the bed and exited the room, returning a few moments later with an older man with graying hair and a ready smile.

"So, I hear you got stuck working with the newbies and one of them didn't do so well on the obstacle course?" he said as he came into the room and gloved up.

"Word travels fast around here," Jeff replied. "The kid forgot to take his pack off before diving beneath the barbed wire." Jeff took a calming breath, still irritated with the kid and with himself for letting his guard down and injuring himself. True, the kid should have obeyed orders and held still, but Jeff should have also been prepared for the worst. He was trained to expect the worst and this time he'd forgotten that.

"Well, we'll get you stitched up and on some antibiotics. You had a tetanus shot before you deployed last time, so there's no need to do that again so soon. When does your team head out again?" the doctor asked, injecting some anesthetic into his arm and quickly stitching up the wounds like a pro.

"Not sure, but I'm thinking we're going to be here for a while. Our last mission ended up going twice as long and a couple of the guys came back with some health issues that need to get cleared up before they can head out again. I'm not keen on taking a partial team anywhere they might send us."

The doctor nodded and then taped a gauze pad over each wound, "I hear that. Well, you know the drill. Keep the wounds clean and dry, no soaking them in water, and you'll need to come back in a week to ten days and have those stitches removed. Any sign of infection or redness, come back right away." He glanced over at the hovering nurse and grinned at her, "Maddie here'll get you fixed up with the right meds. Do you want anything for pain?"

Jeff shook his head, "No, I'll stick with over-the-counter stuff."

"Well, if you change your mind, just give the front desk a call. I'll leave a temporary order there for you, just in case you need it later tonight."

"Thanks, doc." Jeff scooted himself off the bed and prepared to pull his shirt back on, but the nurse was already there with a helping hand. He accepted her help, liking the fresh lemon scent of her hair and wondering what she would say if he were to ask her to dinner. *No better time than right now to find out. Maybe she'll even say yes because you're injured.*

"The pharmacy should already have your prescription ready, if you wanted to stop by and pick it up before you leave."

Jeff nodded and grinned at her, "Thanks, uhm…your name is Maddie?"

She nodded with a smile, "Yes, I guess we never got around to introducing ourselves. Maddie Grantham from Warner Robbins, Georgia."

Jeff shook her outheld hand, "Major Jeff Young, originally from Sandy, Utah, but most recently I've been stationed here."

"Have you been stationed other places as well?" she asked curiously.

Jeff nodded, "Several other bases, but this one is the most recent. We've been operating out of here for almost a year now, not that we really spend much time in the States. Just recovery time and then we're off on another mission."

"Wow! So, how long do most of your missions last?" she asked, walking him towards the pharmacy at the end of the hallway.

"A couple of days to a few weeks. We've had longer missions, but those are usually reconnaissance operations and we know beforehand that we're going to be gone for a month or so."

Maddie said nothing, but greeted the pharmacy technician and then backed away so he could finish his business. She gave him a smile, "I should probably get back to work..."

"Wait!" Jeff stopped her from leaving. "I was wondering...if you don't have any other plans, would you like to have dinner with me tonight?"

Maddie smiled at him and then shyly nodded her head, "I'd like that."

"Great! I know this neat little Italian place off base that makes the best manicotti I've ever tasted. What time do you get off?"

"My shift ends at 6 o'clock..."

"So, is 6:30 good for you?"

Maddie nodded and blushed when Jeff grinned at her, "6:30 sounds perfect. What should I wear?"

"Whatever you want. I'll probably put jeans on since they don't like us going off base in uniform. Draws too much attention and with all of the recent threats these last few years, it's not real safe to be advertising what you do out in the general public."

Maddie nodded and sobered a bit, "I think it's a shame how far things have deteriorated. Where should I meet you?"

"I'll pick you up, just like my daddy taught me to do." Jeff turned back to the pharmacy counter, ignoring the way the technician was watching his interaction with interest. He grabbed a piece of scratch paper and a pen and handed them to her. "Write your address down and I'll find it."

Maddie did so and then handed them back, their fingertips brushing and sending pleasant little tingles up both of their arms. "I really need to get back to work now."

"Go and I'll see you later. I'm really looking forward to it."

Maddie blushed again and smiled, "So am I. Bye." She gave him a little wave and headed back down the hallway.

Jeff turned and gave the pharmacy technician a smile, "That girl doesn't know it yet, but she's gonna marry me."

The technician looked stunned and then stuttered, "But...you just met her...right? I mean, I heard you guys talking and...well, it seems as if you just met."

Jeff grinned, "We did, but my daddy always said when I met the right girl, I'd know. And I know Maddie Grantham is the girl for me. She might not know it yet, but that's what dating is for."

The pharmacy technician handed over his prescription and smiled at him, "Well, good luck to you. I hope everything works out well for both of you."

Chapter 1

Middle of October, Colorado Springs, Colorado ...

Maddie Young walked towards the Army Post Office, silently praying that today would be the day she heard something from Jeff. Her husband. She looked down at the simple gold band adorning the fourth finger of her left hand, just to reaffirm in her own mind that she was truly a married woman. *Yep. There it is, now if only I knew where the man wearing the matching ring happened to be or when he might be back...*

She pushed open the door, nodding and smiling at a few of the other military wives in the waiting area. A quick scan showed that they all had mail in their hands, and Maddie took a deep breath before stepping up to the counter and giving Tamara Jenkins, the mail clerk, a tremulous smile.

"Hey, Maddie," Tamara greeted her with a smile that didn't reach her eyes and Maddie felt her confidence and optimism slip.

"Any mail today?" Maddie went through the motions of asking, already seeing the answer in the other woman's brown eyes.

Tamara gave her a sad look and then slowly shook her head, "I'm afraid not. Maybe tomorrow, though. You come back tomorrow, maybe there will be something then."

Maddie nodded and then turned, seeing that several of the other wives were watching her with sad looks on their faces. She gave them on overly bright smile and headed for the exit, "Y'all have a nice day, now." Her Southern roots came out when she was stressed, and the lack of any communication from her newly married husband, for more than three months, was definitely in that category.

If anyone would have told her she'd find herself in this predicament, she would have laughed in their faces, assured them that what she and Jeff had was more than strong enough to stand up to his deployment, and then proudly displayed the weekly letters he'd sent her. That was how she'd thought about things three months ago. Now...well, her husband had some explaining to do when he finally came back to the States.

She'd heard some of the others talking in whispers right after they'd gotten married. They didn't know her and didn't seem to want to change that. Maddie hadn't let it get to her, pulling upon her Southern roots and proper etiquette to simply return their criticism with kindness and a ready smile.

She'd not known much about the military until moving to Colorado Springs and getting a job as a nurse at the base hospital. They'd been short staffed and as a travelling nurse, she'd been thrilled at the chance to move to Colorado and see the Rocky Mountains. She'd only been there for a few weeks prior to meeting Jeff and their courtship had taken all of five weeks. Looking back now, she didn't regret the speed at which she'd given her heart to Jeff; she just wished she'd been prepared for what his job would require of her. Sighing, she shook her head and determined to find something more positive to dwell upon.

She'd walked away from the post office, needing the exercise after having worked a double shift at the Army hospital the day before. She was a travelling nurse who specialized in pediatrics, and while the Army hospital didn't treat many youngsters, there were enough that she'd been able to find a job right on the base. A permanent job, no less. She'd only had three months left on her contract with the agency who'd placed her in this position, and the Army hospital director had offered her a position she couldn't refuse.

Looking both ways, she crossed the street and then headed for the apartment she was supposed to be sharing with her husband. His stuff was still on the bookshelves and hanging in the closet, but the sheets had long since lost the smell of his cologne, having been washed multiple times in his absence. Maddie always made sure to keep the apartment as clean as possible, hoping each day as she left for work that she'd come home to see him sitting on the couch waiting for her. So far, that hadn't happened.

She crossed another street and headed across the park. She hadn't been eligible for base housing when first coming to Colorado Springs, being as she wasn't actually in the military, but a civilian worker. She'd not been able to find an affordable house, so she'd opted for an apartment. The apartment complex was situated directly across the street from the main compound and therefore, filled completely will military families. She was a block from what she considered home when a green Jeep pulled up to the corner and then waited until she was even with the occupants. She turned her head and smiled at the passenger, "Colonel Lents."

"Mrs. Young. Are you heading home?" The gray-haired man in green fatigues asked her politely.

Maddie nodded her head and then stepped closer to the vehicle, "I am." She paused for a moment, her recent disappointment with Jeff's lack of communication coming to the forefront. She cleared her throat and then slowly and softly asked, "Since you're here, could I ask a question?"

The man lifted a brow and then nodded, "You may ask and I will do my best to answer." He gestured to the young man driving the Jeep to wait, and slid from the vehicle, walking a short ways behind it and then turning to look at her, "What's going on?"

Maddie chose her words carefully, knowing the man was one of Jeff's commanding officers and not wanting to inadvertently get him into trouble. She hadn't been raised around the military and their ways and customs were still very foreign to her. "It's about Jeff...my husband..."

"Yes?"

"Well, he's been gone for three months, and...well, I haven't heard anything from him. Not a letter or an email...nothing."

Colonel Lents looked uncomfortable and walked back to the Jeep. He spoke to the driver, who turned the Jeep off, saluted his commanding officer, and then took off at a jog back the way they'd just come. Colonel Lents slipped into the driver's seat and then waved Maddie forward, gesturing for her to take a seat in the passenger side of the vehicle. "Get in for a minute."

Maddie did so, looking at him and wondering if she'd asked the wrong question. "I'm sorry..."

"Mrs. Young..."

"Maddie, please?" she told him softly.

He nodded his head., "Maddie, I know you and Jeff only had a few days together before he was deployed, but I assumed he'd explained things to you before he left."

"What things?" she asked, feeling as if she'd missed some big piece of the puzzle.

"Jeff's unit...well, they are a covert group. Their missions aren't the kind of thing you'd ever read about in the newspaper, and very few people know the full extent of what they are doing, or even where they are doing it."

Maddie nodded, relieved because Jeff had told her something about this. "I'm aware that he's doing something fairly secretive, but I would have thought he would have been able to contact me...I mean, it's been three months."

"I realize that, but unfortunately, there is nothing I can do to change your current situation."

"Maybe if I could talk to some of the other wives..."

Colonel Lents shook his head. "Maddie, none of the other men in Jeff's unit are married. I'm sure you can begin to understand why."

"None of them are married?" she asked, confused.

"Not any more. Several of them had wives at one point in time, but the demands of their job became too much to bear."

Maddie processed that information, challenging herself to be stronger than those other women. "Can you at least tell me that he's still alive?" she asked, needing some piece of information to give her hope.

"If he wasn't, you would have already been visited by several uniformed officers bearing a letter from the President of the United States and his condolences."

Just hearing his words made Maddie's heart clench painfully. "So, since I haven't been visited thusly, I'm to assume he's still alive and doing well."

"You can assume he's still alive," the Colonel subtly corrected her. He held her gaze and Maddie wished she knew what secrets were lying behind his eyes. After several seconds, she realized he wasn't going to offer her any more information and she briefly wondered if he even knew where Jeff and his teammates currently were.

Maddie nodded and then slid from the vehicle, and then looked at him once more, "How do other people deal with this waiting?"

Colonel Lents gave her a tight smile, "You are doing better than most. My advice would be find something to do off this base so that you're not constantly surrounded by reminders of what you don't know."

Maddie laughed and shook her head, "That might be kind of hard since I work on base at the hospital as well."

"My advice stands. You need to create some time for yourself where you aren't reminded about your lack of information all of the day."

Maddie nodded, "I'll think about that. Thank you for talking to me."

"You are very welcome." He started up the vehicle and Maddie watched him drive away, his advice echoing in her ears. *Something off base that keeps me from thinking about Jeff and his lack of communication all day, every day? Wonder how I'm supposed to do that?*

Chapter 2

Castle Peaks, Montana, February 15th...

Maddie yawned and then stretched her arms up and over her head. She glanced at the clock on the far wall and sighed in relief. The day nurses would be arriving within the hour and then she could head home and catch a few hours of much needed sleep. Yesterday had been Valentine's Day, and as the other nurses were all married, she'd offered to cover the night shift and give them a chance to be with their significant others.

Jess had just given her a look when she'd explained her reasoning, but thankfully she'd not divulged Maddie's private secret to the rest of the nursing staff. Jess had been her roommate before marrying Bryan a few weeks earlier, and she'd discovered the picture Maddie kept on her bedside table shortly after moving in and asked about it.

Yes, I'm married. No, I don't know where my husband is or when he might be coming home. Yes, I miss him, but dwelling on his absence was depressing and since there isn't anything I can personally do to change that situation, I'm focusing on what I can do. Yes, I plan to stay married to him. I just need him to come home!

It was a point of embarrassment for Maddie, and when she'd decided to take Colonel Lents' advice and get off the base for a while, she was sure he hadn't expected her to give him a forwarding address in another state. Maddie had waited for three months for her husband to contact her in some way, but each day that passed with no letters or emails, she became more depressed and more inclined to negative thinking. Maddie didn't want to be that kind of person, so she'd taken steps to do something different. Something positive.

She'd seen the ad for a pediatric oncology nurse in the breakroom at the Army hospital and before she could talk herself out of it, she'd forwarded a letter of interest and her resume to the address at the bottom of the ad. She'd never worked specifically with cancer patients, but she was very good with pediatric patients and would love to work in an environment where she really felt like she was making a difference. Where she could go home at the end of a shift knowing she personally had made a difference in someone's life.

After a phone interview, she'd received an email offering her the position and a generous relocation package as well. She'd not given herself time to think, but gone straight to Colonel Lents' office and provided him with the clinic's address as her new forwarding address until further notice. He'd been shocked that she was going to leave Colorado Springs, but she'd assured him she needed to do this or go crazy worrying. She'd not reminded him that he'd been the one to suggest she find something to do off the base, thinking that wouldn't be very smart on her part.

She'd packed up most of her clothing and a few of her belongings, thankful that she didn't have any live plants or pets to worry about, and left the keys to her and Jeff's apartment with the neighbor down the hall. She had never intended to leave Colorado Springs for good, just long enough to let Jeff finish his mission and come home. Then she'd have to figure out whether she could handle being a military pseudo-widow the next time he was deployed or not. The only way out was with a divorce, but Maddie and Jeff had promised one another they would exhaust all other avenues of reconciliation before they ever let that word enter into their marriage. Maddie had grown up in a loving household, where her parents adored one another, and she'd been thrilled to find a man who wanted that for himself. Maddie wasn't a quitter and it rankled that she'd allowed herself to be put in this position to where she'd even let the word enter her thoughts. In true Maddie fashion, she'd taken her negative thoughts and turned them around. She wasn't content to sit by and let the days and weeks pass her by while she wallowed in self-pity, so she'd done something about it. She'd moved to Castle Peaks, Montana.

Yawning again, she picked up the charts and started on her early morning rounds once more. There were only three kiddos in the pediatric care unit right now, with several more due to arrive to begin their treatments in the next few days. The unit held twenty beds, but since she'd been in Castle Peaks, never had there been any more than a dozen patients in residence. *Thank you, God!*

Cancer was one of the most hateful words she'd ever come across, and when it affected kids, it was brutal and devastating in ways that no amount of faith in God could help explain. Maddie had spent more time praying for her patients in the last five months since taking this position than she'd ever prayed in her life. She'd grown closer to God in the process, but her heart had also suffered some harsh blows along the way, and she knew it was only a matter of time before she had to deal with another heartbreak.

She stopped outside the blue room, all of the rooms being given colors instead of numbers in deference to their young occupants. She took a deep breath and pushed the door open, stopping when she saw Caroline Graves sitting in the rocking chair with Annsley in her lap.

The now five-year-old had osteosarcoma that had travelled throughout her little body before the doctors had figured out what was ailing the small two-year-old. She'd undergone extensive chemotherapy and radiation treatment for the last three years, and the effects on her growth had been tremendous. She looked like a three-year-old in her height and body weight, but she had the sharp mind and depth of compassion of a child much older than five.

Caroline looked up at the squeak of Maddie's shoes on the tiled floor and gave her a tired smile.

"How's she doing?" Maddie asked, hoping she could check the little girl's vitals without waking her up. These days, the only respite Annsley seemed to get from the pain was when she was sound asleep, drug-induced most of the time.

Caroline shook her head. "She's sleeping, but not soundly. The pump is working every six minutes right now."

Maddie nodded her head, biting the inside of her lip to keep from showing how sad that news made her. Annsley wasn't going to survive this latest round of treatment, and everyone seemed to be resigned to that fact. For the last twenty-four hours, she'd been on a morphine pump that automatically dispensed a dose of the pain killer into her IV whenever her pain started to etch up and her heart rate increased. The last patient Maddie has seen get to this stage hadn't lasted more than a day and half before taking their last breath.

"Dr. Jackson will be in for rounds at 7 unless you think I should page him sooner?" Maddie offered, seeing the harsh truth registering in the young mother's eyes. *Her child is dying and there is nothing she can do to stop it. Dear God, why is this happening?*

Caroline shook her head, "There's nothing more that he can do, so don't bother him. He's done so much for us already…I know this is hard on everyone here."

Maddie nodded and gingerly took the little girl's pulse and listened to her heart and lungs. She made a few notations in her chart and then noted the oxygen saturation rate using a finger monitor and wrote down the blood pressure from the machine that automatically recorded it every fifteen minutes.

"Her lungs sound clear right now," Maddie told Caroline. She checked the level in the morphine pump and made a note to order up a replacement from the in-house pharmacy, just in case things continued throughout the day.

"Thank you," Caroline told her, with tears in her eyes.

Maddie cleared her throat, "You are very welcome. Is there anything I can do for you? Anyone I can call?"

Caroline shook her head, "My mom and dad are coming this morning from Illinois. Their fight landed in Bozeman half an hour ago, and they are driving over...my husband got here an hour ago and is getting our other three kids settled into the hospice house."

"Did he arrange for someone to stay with the kids?" Maddie asked, knowing they ranged in ages from just under a year to eight.

"His niece came along; she's fifteen and is going to watch the little ones for us." Caroline's voice broke and Maddie laid a tender hand on her shoulder. "She's missing school, and..."

Maddie squeezed her shoulder and shook her head, "You don't have to talk anymore. Hold your little girl and I'll send Dr. Jackson in as soon as he arrives."

Caroline nodded and dropped her forehead down to rest upon the sleeping little girl's bald head, the treatment having stolen her beautiful golden hair months earlier. She'd been in remission twice over the last three years, but this last time, the cancer had spread rapidly and gotten to her spine before it could be stopped.

Maddie left the room, wiping her tears away before heading down the hallway. She checked on her other two patients, both of whom were either in remission or showing signs that their cancer was on the way to being eradicated. They were the lucky ones who would someday soon leave the cancer clinic and return to being happy and healthy kids. Annsley would never have that opportunity, but Maddie consoled herself that the little girl loved Jesus and soon would be pain free and never have to worry about cancer again.

She finished her charting just as the day nurses started to arrive. She checked in on Annsley once more, and made the day nurses promise to call her if things got much worse before she returned. She was heading home to grab a shower and a few hours of sleep, and then she would return to sit with the young mother and offer as much comfort as she could. It would break her heart, but she prayed as she drove home, that in some small way God could use her to help bring peace to the Graves' family in the midst of their sorrow.

Chapter 3

Same day, Colorado Springs, Colorado…

Major Jeff Young saluted Colonel Lents as he was bid to enter the man's office, and then he stood at attention in front of the large wooden desk, wondering what had been so important that he'd needed to stop here before even going home to see his wife. A woman he'd not seen in almost nine months!

"At ease," Colonel Lents told him, standing and coming around to sit a hip on the corner of his desk. "Welcome back."

"Thank you, sir. It's good to be back in the States," Jeff told him, still standing straight and still.

"I've read your report and was happy to read that you haven't suffered any long-term effects at having been a guest of the enemy for so many weeks."

Jeff clenched his jaws tight, hoping the man didn't want to dig into those weeks too deeply. He'd already been debriefed while in Germany, and he really didn't want to go through it all again. Not yet. He'd survived, but several of his teammates had not, and the guilt he felt for living while they lay buried in some Middle Eastern sand pile was immense.

When he didn't reply, Colonel Lents continued, "You're on mandatory leave for the next three months."

Jeff looked at him in shock and shook his head, "Sir?"

"You heard me, soldier. Many things have happened while you and your team were gone, including the fact that your little wife didn't have a clue what she was getting herself into here. That girl wore a path in the concrete between your apartment and the post office."

Jeff's shoulders sagged, "I wrote her when we got to Germany..." His team had gotten their orders only after leaving the base nine months earlier, and had then inserted themselves deep into enemy territory. It had been a simple grab and snatch mission, designed to gather intel and several key players in the terrorist group currently causing the most problems in the area, but everything had gone sideways from the moment they set foot on the ground. What should have been a simple nine-week mission from start to finish turned into several skirmishes and ended up with his entire team being captured.

Because of their deep cover, it had been several weeks after their capture before their commanding officers had even known there was a problem. By then, they'd been moved and weren't even in the same country as when they'd first landed. Since they weren't supposed to be there in the first place, the military had taken extreme measures to keep their captivity a secret for as long as possible, and had taken several more months of negotiations and the like before they'd made the decision to just send in a covert ops teams to rescue them.

They hadn't planned on the terrorists continuing to move the captives every few weeks, the result being several failed rescue missions before they were finally met with success. That success had come a week earlier, and not a moment too soon. The terrorists had run out of places to move them and Jeff had feared they were all destined to die within days, if not hours, when the world around him had exploded. Hearing the voices of fellow soldiers calling out for him and his team had been the sweetest sound he'd ever heard.

Colonel Lents cleared his throat and Jeff realized he'd allowed his mind to drift for a moment. "My apologies, sir. I must be more tired than I realized."

"Understandable, son."

Jeff nodded, "I did write Maddie...there wasn't an opportunity for me to call, what with the time differences and debriefing...

"You don't have to explain it to me, I understand the logistics better than anyone. Your letter, as heartfelt and needed as it is, probably won't arrive for at least another five days," Colonel Lents finished for him.

Jeff nodded, "I understand. She doesn't know we were coming in today?"

Colonel Lents sent him a look and shook his head, "Someone screwed up and I didn't even know your team was coming in today. I only heard about what happened two weeks ago. Whomever was running this mission needs to look up the words communication and cooperation. I've been kept in the dark, along with your wife."

Jeff could hear the unspoken anger in his commanding officer's voice. He looked him in the eye, "You've seen her?"

Colonel Lents nodded his head. "Not for a while, but yes."

"Begging your pardon, Sir, but I would dearly love to go and see her..."

"That's going to be hard to do, son."

Jeff swallowed and asked, "And why is that?"

"She's not here. She was having a hard time, watching other families being reunited and the like, and I suggested she find something to do off the base to help take her mind off her own lack of information. I was thinking she might join a health club, or pick up a new hobby...She might have taken my suggestion a little too far."

"How's that?" Jeff asked, a muscle ticking in his jaw as he struggled to figure out what he wasn't getting.

"She's in Montana."

"Montana?! What is my wife doing in Montana?" Jeff asked, his voice too loud for the small office and he immediately lowered it and muttered an apology.

"Not necessary, son. Look...Jeff, she took a job at a cancer clinic up there in October..."

"Five months ago? Why didn't I...," he broke off as he realized the timing he was about to question. His team had been surprised and taken captive October 6th. If not for that fateful mission, they would have all been on a plane headed home at the end of the month, if not sooner. Instead, the entire team had been captured, tortured, and used as leverage by the terrorists who hated Americans. Out of the ten men who'd been captured, only six had survived to return home.

"She gave me the address of the clinic before she left and asked me to convey her new address to you when I was able to do so." Colonel Lents handed him a yellow sheet of paper with an address and the name of the facility where she worked, "She's still working there and I'm ordering you to go home and sleep for at least four hours before you attempt to go after her. She's waited this long; another twelve hours or so isn't going to hurt either of you.

"There's a chopper leaving for Bozeman at thirteen hundred hours and I've reserved you a seat on it. You'll need to drive a few hours to get to Castle Peaks, according to the map I looked at online, but the reserve unit up there has a Jeep set aside for your use."

Jeff was stunned and stammered, "I...why are you doing this Sir?"

Colonel Lents gave him a half grin, "Because you took the leap of faith to get married and try to live a normal life, even knowing the odds were against you in this job. That little wife of yours seemed determined to be happy, even though I know how hard it was to leave that post office empty handed, day after day.

"You're a great soldier and you've done more for in the line of duty than many will ever be asked to do. You have more than enough years in to ask for, and receive, a desk post or to just get out and find a normal job that doesn't endanger your life every minute of the day. You need a chance to live as a married man before you decide what direction your future lies. Three months. I'll expect to see papers on my desk at the end of that time frame."

Jeff nodded his head, having a hard time wrapping his head around the gift he'd just been given. While in captivity, he'd promised himself that if he made it out of the desert alive, he was going to go straight to Maddie and find a way to never leave her side again. But the Army was a harsh mistress and his field commander had already been discussing the next mission he and his team would be training for once they reached the base.

He'd not wanted to say anything about his thoughts to the others, but he knew that two of his teammates would never pass their physicals again, allowing them to return to active duty. The other three were already showing signs of PTSD and would have to undergo extensive psychological treatment before they would be cleared to return to duty, if ever. He'd been the only one to escape relatively unscathed, at least in a physical sense. A deliberate act on his captors' part. They'd tortured his teammates, making sure he was within earshot, even going so far as to make him watch at times. For someone in a position of leadership, that had been worse than if they'd been abusing him on a daily basis.

He'd done his best to rid himself of the guilt that came with their deaths, but it still lingered in the back of his mind, rising like an evil shadow in the depths of his sleep. The psychologists he'd spoken with assured him that time would heal those memories and he just needed to keep reminding himself that none of what happened was his fault. Easier said than done, but he was trying. For Maddie, he would keep trying until he had those bad memories conquered. They had no place in his future with the gorgeous redhead he'd swept off her feet so many months prior.

He took his leave of the colonel's office and headed to his apartment. The neighbors all welcomed him back with big smiles, and he told himself that Maddie was simply on a small vacation, and hadn't actually left him. Some of her personal things were still in the apartment, clothes hanging in the closet, and that gave him hope that he could still salvage his marriage.

Their love story was a whirlwind romance of a soldier and the lovely nurse he'd fallen head over heels for the first time he'd seen her smiling face. He'd been helping with the enlisted men's training and when one newbie had gotten himself caught up in some barbed wire on the obstacle course, Jeff had tried to untangle his pack from the wicked wire, only to have the kid – he might have been twenty, maybe…the kid had begun to struggle, thinking he was in trouble and Jeff's arm had gotten sliced by the wire before he could subdue the kid.

He'd needed stitches and that was how he'd met the lovely Maddie. Her red hair and green eyes had called to him, and her Southern drawl had been the sexiest thing he'd heard in a long time. She'd been full of life, and given the amount of death and destruction he'd seen on his team's last mission, it was like seeing the sun come out after a month of rain. He'd been drawn to her like a moth to a flame, and from that day forward, they'd spent part of every day for the next five weeks together.

Their attraction to one another had been instantaneous, not only physical, but they'd connected on a spiritual level. He'd been raised in a Christian household and had always longed to find that one special person God had set aside for him. After spending the last nine years in the service, he'd pushed that dream aside, knowing that men like him didn't find the perfect woman, live in houses with white picket fences, or have the requisite two and a half kids with a dog and cat. He was a military soldier and the job had become his life, to the point where he had trouble remembering what his life had been like before enlisting.

Months of captivity had given him a chance to re-think where his life was headed, and he realized that dream was still there, and he no longer wanted to bury it, but live it. God had seen fit to give him the perfect wife, a woman filled with kindness and compassion for those around her, and a love for life that he desperately needed to survive. Maddie was his wife, and he might have to spend the rest of his years making up the last nine months to her, but he'd do whatever it took to see her smiling for him once again.

But first, he needed sleep and then he needed to be on that chopper. He forced himself to shower and then lay upon the bedspread, closing his eyes and inhaling the gentle fragrance of her perfume that still lingered on the pillows. He rolled over and hugged the pillow tight, finally drifting into an uneasy sleep. He dreamt of seeing Maddie again and holding her close and never letting her go again.

When he boarded the chopper several hours later, he remembered his dreams and prayed that they would become reality before the day was through. *Maddie girl, I'm back and I'm going to make sure you know how much I missed you and how much I need you in my life. Castle Peaks might have taken you away for the last several months, but nothing can take you away from my love. I'm coming up there to prove it.*

Chapter 4

Later that afternoon…

Maddie pushed through the doors of the clinic, mustering up a smile for the security guard and then spying Sara Harding and her sister Grace standing in the foyer. Sara hugged her sister and then turned and headed for the elevators, but something about the other woman caused Maddie to pause and watch her for a moment. She'd only met the woman a few times, and she'd immediately liked everything about her.

Grace was married to Dr. Michael Simpson, the director and chief physician at the Mercer-Brownell Foundation San Diego clinic. They specialized in kids with rare cancers and most of the Castle Peaks kiddos came by referral from them. She was currently visiting her sister, and Maddie knew she was slated to return home in the next few days. Grace spied her and then waved her over as she settled on a seat in the foyer, looking slightly green around the gills and exhausted.

Maddie joined her, concern in her voice when she asked, "Is everything alright?"

Grace nodded and then placed a hand over her stomach, "Everything is fine, except this little one is going to make my life miserable for the next eight months."

Maddie smiled, "You're pregnant?" When Grace grinned broadly and nodded, Maddie's smiled broadened, "Congratulations!"

"Thanks, but since I just found out, and haven't even had time to tell my husband, would you mind keeping it quiet?"

Maddie nodded her head, "Of course. Is Dr. Simpson with you this trip?"

Grace once again shook her head, "No, he brought me up here and then took off for some conference in Chicago. He'll be back tomorrow and then the day after we'll head back to San Diego."

Maddie smiled, "I bet you're ready to get out of the cold and snow."

Grace nodded her head, "To tell you the truth, the beach and some sunshine sound really good about now. Daniella might not agree, but then again, she's still young."

Maddie looked around, "Where is she?" The little girl had stolen everyone's heart upon her first visit, and Maddie had heard all about her exploits and logic from the other employees.

Grace sighed, "She's with Tory and Emily today. They were supposed to go sledding, but Jackson had an emergency here and so they're making snowmen instead."

Maddie's heart tripped a beat hearing Jackson's name and realizing she was back here so soon for the same emergency. Her smile faltered and she moved a step away, "Is he upstairs already, do you know?"

"I'm sure he is. Tory couldn't tell me what the emergency was because the girl's parents were standing right there, but she looked really sad."

Maddie nodded, "One of our patients is dying. A little five-year-old with bone cancer." She broke off as tears clogged her throat.

Grace stood up and Maddie could see the sheen of tears in her eyes, "She's not going to make it?"

Maddie shook her head quickly, "No." She cleared her throat, "I should probably get upstairs. I want to sit with Caroline and her husband...I don't know what I can do, but maybe just offer them support and a shoulder to cry upon."

Grace walked with her towards the elevators, "Do you mind if I accompany you?"

Maddie looked at her and asked, "Can I ask why you want to?"

Grace gave her a shake of her head, "I can't really answer that, but maybe there's something I could do to help ease their pain. When Sara's and my mom was sick, sometimes she would ask me to sing to her...it always made her smile and helped calm her down so the pain medication could work."

Maddie stepped into the elevator and gestured for Grace to join her, "Annsley...that's the little girl's name...loves music. Her mom almost always has something playing on the small stereo they brought from home."

"Do you know what kind of music she likes to listen to?" Grace asked.

Maddie nodded her head, "She likes just about anything. Her mom often plays the old hymns at night...I think they bring her comfort."

"As they are supposed to. Do you think they would let me sing for them?" Grace asked and Maddie's eyes filled with tears. She nodded, unable to get words past a throat that had closed up with emotion.

The elevator doors opened and Maddie immediately realized that time was short. The hallway had been blocked off so that other patients and visitors wouldn't intrude upon the family currently saying goodbye to their little girl in the blue room, and the nurses all looked teary eyed.

Maddie stopped by the nurse's desk and quickly looked at the latest chart readings before taking a deep breath and heading towards the room with Grace by her side. Soft music was playing as she pushed the door open to see Caroline Graves sitting on the small settee by her husband, their daughter cradled between their arms, her eyes closed in sleep for the moment.

Caroline looked up and met Maddie's eyes, tears running unchecked down her cheeks. Maddie quietly introduced Grace and then sat down on one of the two remaining chairs, silently praying for peace and comfort to fill the small room.

Dr. Jackson Myers sat on the other side of the room, his expression one of sorrow and defeat. He loved each and every one of his patients as if they were his own children, and losing one always caused him, and everyone else at the clinic, to grieve their loss. He met Maddie's eyes and then passed her the child's most recent results.

Maddie read the report that indicated the cancer had reached Annsley's brain stem, and she knew her initial assumption, that today could be the day Annsley finally found freedom from her pain and suffering, was more than likely at hand. The brain stem controlled the bodily functions that kept one alive – heartbeat, breathing… when it stopped functioning, Annsley's body would as well.

Caroline wiped her tears and then drew from a well of strength somewhere deep inside herself. "Annsley woke up a bit ago and asked for you," she told Maddie.

Maddie bit her lip and nodded, "I'm sorry I wasn't here for her."

Clark Graves shook his head, "Don't be. She was only awake for a few minutes and then the morphine kicked in."

Maddie nodded again, "Still, I wish I could have been here for her."

Caroline gave her a sad smile, "You've been here for her, don't ever think you haven't." She started to say something else, but

Annsley started fidgeting and moments later she opened up her baby blue eyes and looked up at her parents with a small smile. "Daddy…"

"I'm here, baby girl. Daddy's right here."

"It doesn't hurt anymore."

"That's good, honey. Just rest and let the medicine…"

"No, daddy. It's not the medicine. Is Maddie here?"

Maddie stood up and approached the settee, "I'm right here, sweetie. I heard you were asking for me."

Annsley tried to nod her head, but she didn't have any strength left, "I have a message for you."

"A message?" Maddie asked, confused and curious.

Annsley tried to lift her hand, and Maddie reached out and clasped it in her own, "What message, sweetie?"

"Jesus told me I had to come back and tell you…"

"You talked to Jesus?" Maddie asked, goosebumps covering her arms. She'd heard of people having visions and such in their last days, even saying they'd gone to heaven and been sent back for one reason or another, but she'd never encountered it herself. Dr. Jackson was now standing beside her, taking Annsley's vitals, and even Grace had risen and was standing next to her.

Caroline and Clark Graves didn't look alarmed at all, but simply held their daughter as she continued to speak.

"Jesus said that your waiting was over. Maddie, what have you been waiting for?"

Maddie heard the words and her mind immediately went to her husband and the fact that she hadn't heard anything from him for nine long months. "Thank you for giving me that message." She could barely get the words out around the new tears that threatened to break free.

Annsley smiled at her and then looked at Grace and asked softly, "Will you sing to me?"

Grace looked surprised, "How do you know I can sing?"

Annsley didn't answer her; she simply closed her eyes and her face relaxed. Maddie looked at Grace and nodded her head, "Sing for her." She wasn't quite sure what was going on in this room, but the presence of the Great Creator was definitely felt and an atmosphere of peace seemed to be everywhere.

Dr. Jackson looked at Grace and nodded, "Her pulse is slowing down."

Caroline and Clark held each other as they held their daughter and Grace softly started to sing her own rendition of *"Go Rest High on That Mountain."* Maddie cried openly as the little girl slowly slipped away as the last phrase of the song rang out in the room, her heart beating no more. Caroline and Clark kissed their daughter and then allowed Dr. Jackson to place her back on the hospital bed as he quietly notated her time of death.

Maddie hugged the grieving couple and then stepped from the room as the other nurses arrived to begin preparing the body to be removed and prepared for the journey back to her hometown where she would be buried next to her grandparents. Caroline and Clark thanked everyone, leaving a short time later to go tell their other children the sad news, and Maddie found herself needing to be alone with her pain. She thanked Grace for the beautiful homegoing she'd provided the little girl, and then she headed towards the small chapel in the other side of the clinic.

So many emotions were clouding her vision, as were tears that she never saw the man climbing from the military Jeep, nor did she hear him calling her name. She pushed her way inside the building and almost ran down the deserted hallway, turning towards the chapel located at the end of the hallway. She pushed through the stained glass and wooden doors, walking to the front and collapsing on the red plush carpet, giving way to the body wracking sobs she'd barely managed to hold at bay. She cried for Annsley, for Annsley's parents and siblings, and for herself. So much grief. So much heartache. *Dear Lord, why?*

Chapter 5

One hour earlier...

It was late afternoon when Jeff finally drove into the small town of Castle Peaks. He'd activated the GPS app on his cell phone upon leaving Bozeman a few hours earlier, but his battery was down to six percent and it wasn't loading anything correctly. He decided to stop at the first business he found open and ask where he might find the Mercer-Brownell Foundation. The town had a population sign indicating one thousand four hundred and three people lived in the town. It had been changed multiple times in recent days, and given those numbers, he figured everyone in town would know how to reach the cancer clinic.

He was still reeling from the idea that his wife had been so terribly unhappy at the Army base that she'd taken a job elsewhere. He might have understood her taking a job at another hospital in the city, but moving to another state? That was mind boggling and he had spent a considerable portion of the chopper ride to Bozeman praying that she hadn't left him when she'd left her previous job.

The first place he came to in town was the local drugstore. He parked the military Jeep in front of the store, took a quick glance in the rearview mirror, and then headed inside. An older man with white hair was wiping down an old-fashioned countertop and Jeff felt kind of like he'd gone back in time. Black and white tile, laid in a checkerboard pattern, greeted his feet, and the candy counter reminded him of his childhood days.

"Good afternoon, young man," the older man greeted him with a smile. "You're not from around here."

Observant. Jeff smiled and nodded, "No, I'm not. I'm actually looking for someone. She works at the Mercer-Brownell cancer clinic." He watched in alarm as the friendly smile on the older man's face faded and wariness took its place. *What did I say?*

"Does this person know you're looking for them?" the older man asked, suspicion evident in his voice.

Jeff shook his head, "No, but she'll be happy to see me." *I hope.* "My phone's almost dead and I was wondering if you could give me directions…"

The older man shook his head, "No, I'm afraid I can't do that. I'd be happy to call over to the clinic and let this person know you're in town and looking for them."

Jeff didn't like the vibes he was picking up from the older man and he slowly shook his head, "I'd rather just surprise them." In his line of work, he was used to depending on his intuition, and red flags were starting to rise the longer he stayed in the drugstore. *Something here doesn't add up.*

He started to say something else, to maybe introduce himself and see if he could ease the older man's unwarranted wariness, but the bells hanging over the front door jingled as another person entered the store.

Jeff turned and met the blue gaze of the local sheriff, the Silver Star gleaming brightly on the left side of his khaki shirt. The man was eyeing him carefully, and Jeff found himself standing up straight and refusing to flinch beneath the man's stare.

"Jeb," the sheriff addressed the older man.

The older man came around the counter and gave the newcomer a relieved look. "Sheriff, this young man is looking for the clinic. He's here to surprise someone…maybe you'd have time to help him out?"

Jeff could hear something in the older man's voice, and he turned to the sheriff. "Is there a problem here? I just need directions to the clinic."

The sheriff shrugged his shoulders. "Well, as to a problem, you tell me. Who are you here to see?"

Jeff looked at the man and held onto his temper. "My wife. Maddie Young."

The older man gasped and the sheriff looked at him curiously. "Maddie Young has a husband?"

Jeff nodded and extended his hand. "Major Jeff Young at your service. I've been deployed the last nine months and only arrived back in Colorado Springs early this morning to find out that she'd taken a job here."

The sheriff and older man shared a look and then the sheriff took a step forward. "You'll have to forgive Jeb here. We had a psycho stalker a few months back who followed one of the nurses up here all the way from Florida. We've become a little paranoid of newcomers looking for people these days."

Ah, they're acting as protectors. Can't take issue with that. Jeff nodded, "I can understand that. I just want to see my wife. She doesn't even know I'm back in the States…"

The sheriff held out his hand, "Trent Harding. My wife's the director up at the clinic. I'm heading that way now, so why don't you follow me?"

"Sounds good," Jeff agreed, giving the older man a smile. "No hard feelings."

"Sorry about the paranoia, but the last guy made the entire town look over their shoulders."

"You were trying to protect those people at the clinic, and for that, I'm grateful. Anyone who tries to protect others has my

41

respect." Jeff tipped his chin towards the man and then turned to the sheriff, "I'll follow you."

Fifteen minutes later, Jeff pulled into the parking lot of the clinic, coming alongside the sheriff's vehicle and rolling down the passenger window, "Thanks for leading the way up here."

"No problem. I'm heading over to the main building. Any idea what your wife is doing here?"

"She's a pediatric nurse."

"Then she's probably one of the newer nurses on the kids' side of the facility. Follow this parking lot up to the building and then around to the left. The main door to the kids' clinic is on the opposite side of the building."

"Thanks."

"I'll be in the director's office for the next hour or so. If your wife isn't working today, come find me and I'll help you locate her."

Jeff nodded and then put the Jeep back into gear, driving around the second building slowly and smiling as he imagined Maddie's reaction when she first saw him. He hoped she would smile and run into his arms, forgiving him the fact that he hadn't been in a position to contact her, but doubts began to creep in. In reality, he'd only known Maddie for a total of six weeks, they'd spent more time apart in the last year, than together, and it took all of his self-control to force the negative thoughts of what might happen away.

He parked the Jeep next to the curb and was just stepping out of the Jeep when he spied a woman with red hair hurrying from the building. He blinked and realized the woman was his wife, and he called to her, but her head was down, her arms wrapped defensively around her middle, and she was almost running in her haste to reach the other building.

He slammed the door to the Jeep and took off after her, calling her name, but she didn't appear to hear him and never once turned her head in his direction. She disappeared inside the building and by the time he pulled the glass doors open, the hallway in front of him was completely empty. He stepped inside and took a moment to calm his breathing down and appear in control. He walked slowly down the hallway, glancing into each open room in hopes of finding Maddie, but he reached the end of the hallway with no sign of her.

He looked both ways, wishing someone would come along that he could question, but so far everything was very quiet and almost as if this part of the building was empty. He was still trying to decide which way he should go, when the sound of muffled crying came to him from the double wooden doors to his right. The stained glass in the doorways led him to believe this room held some sort of chapel, and he headed that way without a second thought.

When he pulled the doors open and his eyes had adjusted to the dim lighting, he saw the source of the sobbing and his heart broke. *Dear Lord, she's crying as if her heart is breaking.*

He stepped forward and all of the visions he'd had of his homecoming with her dissipated like fog when it encounters the sun. He whispered her name, "Maddie?"

She didn't give any indication of having heard him so he walked towards the front of the room. "Maddie?" he said her name again, squatting down so that he was only a foot away from her. "Sweetheart, please..."

Maddie heard him this time and lifted her head, her eyes swollen and red from her tears, her mouth widening in shock as she looked up at him. She looked like she was going to say something as she struggled to get to her feet, but as Jeff reached to help her up from the floor, she swayed and her eyes rolled back in her head. *She just fainted. What on earth has happened to her?*

Chapter 6

Maddie slowly came back to consciousness, instantly becoming aware of the fact that she was not alone. She tried to open her eyes, but they were heavy still and her mind was working overtime as the second before she'd passed out flashed before her eyes. *Jeff! Jeff was here!*

She forced herself to breathe deeply and then she opened her eyes to see her husband looming over her, his eyes closed and his lips silently moving as if he were praying. "Jeff?" she whispered his name, lifting a hand and reaching for his cheek. *Is he really here? God, please don't let this just be a dream.*

"Maddie? Sweetheart, say something," he whispered to her, clutching her hand to his cheek and rubbing it against his skin. "Please, God...please..."

Maddie watched him for a long moment, taking in his appearance and closed eyes and as he continued whisper her name, she realized he hadn't heard her say his name. His eyes were closed and he she reached up with her other hand and touched his other cheek, "I can't believe it's you," she searched his face, fresh tears filling her eyes, but this time in joy.

His eyes popped open and then crinkled in the corners at the sound of her voice, "Oh, Maddie! You scared me. First, I find you sobbing your eyes out, and then you passed out on me."

Maddie swallowed and then pushed until he helped her to a sitting position, "What are you doing here?" The question sounded so insane, but it was the first thing that came to her mind. This wasn't how she'd envisioned greeting her husband after all these long months, but then again, she'd not known he was even back in the States. *Why hadn't she known he was coming home? Had Colonel*

Lents lost her contact information? What if Jeff hadn't just gotten back and had been searching for her? Questions rushed through her brain, confusing her and taking her focus away from the fact that her husband was squatting down right beside her, looking so handsome and good to her, she had to touch him once more to assure herself he was real and not just a figment of her tired imagination.

Jeff looked at her and then reached for her left hand, his fingers immediately seeking out her ring finger and a frown forming on his face when he found her finger bare. He looked down to confirm what his hands had already felt and then he looked at her, a wounded look in his eyes. "Why?"

Maddie followed his eyes and felt her heart skip a beat. He looked hurt and confused and she hurried to try and explain. She took a breath, "I didn't want to have to answer a bunch of questions when I came here, especially when I didn't know the answers. If I'd worn my ring, my co-workers would have wanted to know where you were, and I couldn't stand the idea of having to tell them I didn't know." She paused for a moment, and then asked, "How long have you been back?"

Jeff looked at her hand again and then took a breath, "We landed at Fort Carson early this morning. Colonel Lents called me into his office as I was leaving the tarmac and told me I would find you here. He arranged a chopper to Bozeman for me as well."

He looked at her, saw the remnants of her tears and the deep sorrow in her eyes, but she also was so beautiful it took his breath away. She'd not changed much while he'd been away, except that her hair was much longer, and currently coming out of the clips she'd used to hold it back on the sides of her head.

He reached a hand out for her and when she only hesitated for a second before crawling the few inches that would bring her into his arms, he closed his eyes, breathed in the fresh lemon scent of her hair and offered up a whispered and heartfelt, "Thank God."

He held her and Maddie reveled in the feel of her husband's arms once more wrapped around her. She stayed there for long moments and then she pushed away from his hold and searched his eyes. "I have so many questions, I don't even know where to start."

Jeff smiled down into her eyes and then sobered, "First things first, tell me why you were so distraught when I walked in here. I watched you leave the other building and called to you, but you didn't hear me. Did someone hurt you? Are you sick?"

Maddie looked down and he watched as her countenance fell. She had so much compassion inside of her and in the few weeks they'd known each other before getting married, he'd seen her invest not only her time and knowledge into her patients, but also her humanity. When she gave him her explanation, his heart broke for the sorrow she was feeling so acutely.

"One of my patients, a little five-year old girl, died a few moments ago. She spent more time in hospitals, fighting to beat the cancer that was eating away at her body, than she did enjoying life as a healthy and happy little girl." She started to cry again, and Jeff pulled her back into his arms.

"It's okay to cry. Go ahead. I'm not going anywhere." *God, please comfort her right now. It kills me to see her so upset.*

Maddie stayed in his arms and allowed herself the freedom to cry once more. She was so glad Jeff was back and he appeared to be in good health, but there was a something in his eyes she couldn't name that scared her. After a long while, all cried out and feeling much calmer, she lifted her head and met his eyes again, "Thank you."

"You don't have to thank me. You should probably be furious with me." Jeff took a bracing breath, ready for her to unleash her righteous and rightly placed anger firmly at his feet. He'd know their first separation while he was deployed would be tough on her, but

46

he'd never thought to prepare her for one that might last in excess of nine months. He and his team would have been hard pressed to imagine a mission that could have gone so terribly wrong. But it had and know he was back and had to figure out how to piece together the life he'd left behind. He knew for certain, more so after seeing Maddie once again, that whatever that life looked like, he wanted her to be right there with him. *But could she deal with what had happened?* Her next words floored him.

Maddie shook her head, "Why would I be furious with you?"

He gave her an incredulous look and then brusquely answered her. "Because I abandoned you," Jeff told her, hating the sound of the words.

Maddie was quiet for a moment and then asked, "Could you have contacted me during the last nine months?"

Jeff shook his head. "No, but that doesn't matter."

"Of course, it does," she told him fiercely. "Why are you so ready to take guilt that doesn't belong to you? The military sent you away and I know you would have come back sooner, or written or called, if you could have."

"But you left Colorado Springs and moved to Montana," he reminded her.

Maddie nodded her head, "I needed to. I loved working at the base hospital, don't get me wrong; but every day I went to the post office, and I saw the pitying looks the other military wives gave me...even the post office clerk pitied me, and I knew if I stayed in that situation I would end up wallowing in self-pity and depressed. That's not who I am or how I wanted to be. Colonel Lents suggested I find something away from the base to do."

She paused for a moment, remembering the shock on the man's face when she'd given him her forwarding address, "I don't think he expected me to take his suggestion quite this far, but I was needed here and I felt useful once again. I thought about you every single day, but having something meaningful to do with my hands and my time lessened the worry and kept me from thinking about how long you'd been gone."

Jeff listened to her and then pulled her back into his arms, grateful when she came willingly, "I missed you so much. I don't know what I did to deserve you, but thank you for not giving up on me. We should have been back months ago, but things went haywire, and I can't tell you too much because the entire mission was off the books..."

"What does that mean, exactly?" Maddie asked.

"It basically means the government sent us over there but only a few people knew where we were going or what our true mission was. Needless to say, the lines of communication were not as thorough as they should have been and we ended up...my team and I...getting captured by the very people we were trying to surveil."

"You were captured?" Maddie asked, pushing away from him and quickly scanning his body for injuries. "How long? What did they do to you? Are you injured?"

"Whoa!" Jeff told her, clasping her wandering hands as she tried to check him out. "To answer your questions...Too long. I fared the best out of all the team...," his voice faltered as he remembered the four men who had given their lives over there. "I lost four friends and teammates while we were held captive. As for injuries, I'm fine."

Maddie had a million questions running through her brain, but there was something in her voice that told her he was having trouble just getting the basic words out and her insisting he go into detail was something he wasn't prepared to deal with. Not right now. Maybe never, but she vowed to be there for him whenever he was ready to discuss what had happened.

In the meantime, she was so happy he was back, now that it was finally registering in her brain, she wanted to jump up and down and shout to the heavens, but sorrow over Annsley's death kept her silent and still. The little girl's words came back to her and she gasped, "Annsley gave me a message just before she died."

"A message? Is Annsley the little girl?" Jeff asked.

Maddie nodded, "Do you believe the stories you've heard about people visiting heaven or talking with God and then coming back before they died?"

Jeff was quiet for a few seconds and then nodded his head, "I guess I have to. It's plausible, and some of the people…like that little girl who died and then came back to life and told about meeting her little sister who died in the womb and her grandparents who died before she was born…they're just too *real* to not believe they're true."

Maddie nodded, "I believe them as well, even more so after today. Annsley told me my waiting was over and the only thing I could think of that I've been waiting for was you to come back home."

Jeff was shocked, "She told you that? When?"

"Just a little while ago. Right before she died, actually." She looked up at Jeff, "There's only a few people who even know I'm married here. Annsley wasn't one of them. I never discussed you or what brought me to Castle Peaks with her."

"So, you're thinking this message was from God?"

Maddie slowly nodded, "Yes. Does that sound strange to you?"

Jeff shook his head, "Not at all. After the last few weeks, nothing surprises me anymore."

"What happened?" she asked, watching him closely.

Jeff sighed, "Suffice it to say that if our rescue team had been two minutes later, I probably wouldn't be with you now. One day I'll tell you about some of the things that happened while we were in captivity, but right now, I want to focus on more positive things. Is that alright with you?"

Maddie nodded, "That's alright with me." She snuggled into his arms once more, wrapping her arms around his chest and inhaling his scent. *He's still wearing the same cologne.*

Jeff smoothed her hair back after removing the remaining clips she'd used after her nap earlier and gave her a lopsided grin, "I love sitting here with you, catching up and such, but do you think we could move this somewhere not on the ground." His body wasn't quite recovered yet and sitting on the ground with her had caused his legs to start cramping and he feared if he stayed in that position much longer he'd make a fool of himself when he finally did try to get up.

Maddie nodded and pushed away from him, intending to get to her feet, but while she'd been on the ground, her legs hadn't fared much better and had fallen partially asleep and were refusing to function correctly. Without a thought for his presence of where she was, she didn't seem worried about how silly she might look as she turned onto her hands and knees and crawled to the first row of pews and used them to push herself upwards. Jeff gained his own feet and was right there, lifting her the rest of the way as she stumbled, "Whoa! I've got you."

Maddie nodded and once she was sure she could stand on her own, she smiled up into his twinkling eyes, "Thanks. I guess I was on the floor a lot longer than I thought."

"Trust me, holding you is never a hardship," Jeff told her. "Shall we get out of here, or do you have something else you need to do first?"

Maddie shook her head, "I worked the nightshift and only came back to say farewell to Annsley and support her parents. I should probably let the desk nurses know I'm leaving the premises though. I'm not on until tomorrow morning." She glanced at the watch on her wrist and couldn't believe it was already going on 6 o'clock in the evening. She had the next day off to catch up on her sleep before she returned to the day shift. "Do you want to come with me?"

Jeff nodded and placed a hand upon her lower back as they headed down the red carpeted aisle. "Do you have a vehicle?" she asked as they exited the chapel and headed for the exit to the building.

"Colonel Lents arranged for me to use one of the Reserve Jeeps. It's parked out at the curb. Do you have your car here?"

Maddie nodded, "Yes." She pushed open the door, her mind going in a variety of different directions. *What do I have at the apartment I can fix for dinner? Does he have to go right back to Colorado Springs? Why am I so nervous? We're married after all, it's not like he's a complete stranger. God, help me out here. Please?*

Chapter 7

As Maddie stepped in the children's side of the clinic, she felt her face flush as everyone turned and watched the handsome man right beside her. Jeff was tall, almost 6'3", with broad shoulders, piercing eyes that were more gray than they were blue, and the physique that told everyone around he wasn't someone they wanted to mess with. His close cropped haircut and the hint of muscle beneath the t-shirt visible under his leather jacket gave him a dangerous air that was hard to ignore.

Maddie could feel his hand at her lower back and he was walking close enough for her to feel the heat coming off of his body. He bent down and whispered in her ears, "Everyone's looking at us."

She turned her head and with an impish smile, she told him, "Correction. Everyone is looking at you."

"Great, that makes it so much better." Jeff gave her a rueful grin and then stepped a bit closer when she stopped in the hallway.

"They're all very nice, just a little protective of their own." Maddie looked over her shoulder at him and felt her heart flutter at his nearness. They were man and wife, but he'd been gone so long…a flurry of nerves and excitement had her heart beating a fast rhythm and butterflies circling inside her belly. *Jeff's back!*

"And do they consider you one of their own?" Jeff whispered.

His comment brought her back to the present and she looked up to see Jess standing at the nurse's station, watching her with a look of stunned belief and curiosity on her face. She knew her friend was going to want some answers and soon.

"Where'd you go?" Jeff whispered for her ears alone.

She looked up at him and shook her head, "Nowhere."

Jeff grinned, his expression saying he knew she was having trouble staying focused now that the shock of his arrival was starting to wear off, and he asked again, "So? Do these people staring at me like I have two heads consider you one of them?"

Maddie nodded, a warm feeling filling her chest as she recognized the truth of that statement. "Yes. They've become like a second family." They had been her saving grace these last several months. Not only had they provided her a nurturing and engaging work environment, but they'd offered her their friendship and support without expecting much in return. She'd come to Castle Peaks trying to find something to keep her mind and heart occupied until her husband's return, and she'd found a place that had done all of that and more.

"I'm glad you found that here...I never imagined how staying at the base would make you feel. I guess I'm kind of surprised you didn't go back home."

Maddie shook her head, "Let's not go into that right now? Okay?" She couldn't have gone back home with a ring on her finger, knowing that her parents hadn't been invited to the wedding, and with no idea of when they might get the privilege of meeting her new husband. She wouldn't do that to them, nor would she do that to his parents. As far as she knew, neither set of parents knew what was happening with their children, and Maddie had been content to let things lie for the time being.

Jeff searched her eyes and then nodded. "Sure. We don't have to discuss those things right now. Why don't you finish up and then maybe we can go grab some dinner? I saw a diner in town..."

Maddie immediately shook her head. Going to the diner with Jeff would only serve to fuel the gossip network that was alive and well in Castle Peaks. It wasn't always a negative thing, and the townsfolk wouldn't discuss her affairs with any ill intentions meant, but she didn't want to share her time with Jeff. She didn't know how long he had, or when he would have to return to Colorado Springs. She didn't want to waste one minute of it. "How about we just go back to my apartment? I could fix us something to eat and we could talk…"

Jeff nodded and smiled at her, "That sounds really good, hon. In fact, that's the best suggestion I've heard in months."

Maddie smiled at him and then turned to take care of her business. She stepped away from him and approached the nurse's station, "I'm going to head home…"

Jess stepped up to her side and nudged her shoulder, whispering so that the other nurses couldn't hear her question. "Is that your husband?"

Maddie looked at her and nodded, "Yes. He's back."

"I can see that. You look like you've been crying. Is everything okay?"

Maddie nodded and sighed, "Annsley's death got to me and he arrived just as I was heading towards the chapel. He found me there…"

"How did he get here?" Jess asked, sneaking a peek at the handsome man over her shoulder.

"He said his team got back into Colorado Springs early this morning and his CO arranged a flight to Bozeman for him. He drove straight up here from there to see me."

Jess wrapped and arm around her shoulders, "I'm so happy for you. This is what you've been waiting for."

Maddie nodded, "It is, but now that he's here…well, I'm nervous."

Jess gave her a sympathetic look, "Of course you are. He's been gone for so many months…"

"Yes, but it's also…what if he wants me to go back with him? He'll deploy again, and I'll be back in the same boat as I was before. I can't…I don't want to be all alone again. I don't want to throw in the towel, but honestly, I don't know if I could handle him leaving again…" Maddie heard herself complaining and closed her eyes at how pathetic she sounded. *Some military wife you're turning out to be. Where's your stiff upper lip and positive outlook on life now? Come one, get it together. You knew this was Jeff's life when you married him. You can't complain now, what's done is done.*

"You need to stop overthinking this right now," Jess advised her. "Take it one day at a time…from what you told me, you and he didn't have that much time together as a couple before he shipped out. Get to know one another all over again. How long is he staying for?"

Maddie looked at her and then shook her head, "I don't know." She couldn't remember if Jeff had told her his future plans or not. *Dear Lord, how long will he be here? Are they going to send him out again right away? What does he expect from me?*

Jess smiled at her and hugged her once more, "Well, don't worry about that for now. He's here tonight and you need to get out of here and go spend some time with him."

Maddie nodded, "Yeah. About Annsley…"

Jess shook her head, sobering. "Her parents have already made arrangements for the body to be taken back to their hometown. They're at the hospice house with their other kiddos…I don't expect them to be back until it's time to sign for her body."

"I hate this part of our jobs," Maddie told her with a voice full of emotion.

Jess nodded her head, "I'm with you on that one." She closed the chart she was writing in just as the elevator dinged and Bryan and Trent both stepped off. The men joined Jess and Maddie at the nurse's station and Maddie waved Jeff over and started to make introductions.

"Jess, I'd like you to meet my husband, Jeff Young."

Jess smiled at him and shook his hand, "Thank you for your service to this great country. Not everyone is so willing to sacrifice in that way."

Maddie watched as Jeff flushed and nodded, "No thanks needed. You work with Maddie?"

"I was her roommate before I got married." Jess pulled Bryan over. "This is my husband, Bryan and this is…"

"We've already met," Jeff assured her, shaking Trent's hand and then Bryan's. "Nice to meet you."

"You as well. I'm glad to see that you completed your mission and returned to the States. Maddie here has been a trouper about you being gone. In fact, most people don't even know you exist."

Maddie blushed, "I just didn't want to answer a bunch of questions I didn't have the answers to."

Jeff stepped in and placed a hand on her lower back, "It's okay, hon. You don't have to make excuses for me." He met the others' eyes and explained, "My team has never been gone this long on a mission. What was supposed to be routine turned into a complete and utter disaster along the way."

Bryan gave him a critical look and then asked, "Special Forces?"

Jeff nodded, "Kind of."

"Black ops?" Bryan asked, with a raised brow.

"That would be a closer description. I can't really say much more."

Bryan shook his head, "You don't need to. I just recently got out of the FBI after being in deep cover for a couple of years."

"You got out?" Jeff asked, curiosity in his voice.

"Yeah. We should get together and talk. Trent and I are headed up to do some ice fishing at the lake tomorrow. Why don't you tag along?"

Jeff blinked and looked uncertain, but Maddie came to his rescue, "You should do that so I don't feel guilty coming to work. I'm on day shift tomorrow."

"Really? I don't know...I haven't been ice fishing in a number of years."

"It's like riding a bike," Trent told him with a smile.

"Yeah, probably. Sure...why not?"

"Great!" Trent and Bryan both grinned at him. Trent gave them all a quick wave of his fingers and then headed for the exit, "I've got to go help Sara with the girls. I love being a dad!"

Bryan watched him go with a smile, "He really does like being a dad. I need to get out of here as well. I'm taking the evening shift, so I'll see you tomorrow," he told Jeff, and then he kissed Jess, "And I'll see you a bit later. Wait up for me."

"You know I will," she replied with a grin and Jeff couldn't help but smile at the love the two people obviously shared. He looked down at Maddie and saw that she was watching her friend as well. *Time for me to start acting like a husband and give her something else to smile about.*

Chapter 8

Later that evening...

Maddie had found a package of chicken in the freezer, and after quickly thawing it, she'd made Jeff a typical Southern meal of fried chicken, mashed potatoes, and corn. She'd remembered his liking for Southern style sweet tea and had quickly made him some, moving about her small kitchen nervously, until he pulled her to a stop in front of him and made her take a deep breath.

"Maddie, I know this feels awkward...I've been gone so long..."

She gave him a tremulous smile, "I don't know what's wrong with me..."

He smiled down into her eyes, "I know something that might help." Without saying another word, he dipped his head and kissed her gently on the lips. He didn't rush the action, nor did he pull back right away. He stayed there, savoring the moment, and only when she moved closer to him and wrapped her arms around his neck did he deepen the kiss and let her feel just how badly he'd missed her while gone.

He kissed her lips and then her eyes and let his lips travel across her jawline to where her neck and shoulder met. She tipped her head back and gave him access, her hands clutching at his neck and the back of his t-shirt the entire time.

"There were days I didn't think I would ever hold you in my arms again," he murmured against her shoulder.

"You're here now. That's what matters most to me," she assured him, but Jeff wasn't positive that would always be the case. At some point, she'd want to know what had happened to him and his team, and he was afraid that when he refused to give her the answers, she'd hold it against him.

Jeff kissed her once more and then she pushed out of his arms and resumed fixing their dinner, her movements more relaxed and her countenance less tight that a few minutes before. He sighed and took a seat at the small bar area, "Did you ever tell your parents about us?"

Maddie looked up at him and then blushed and shook her head, "No. I knew how sad my mama would be that I got married without inviting her and my dad, and then one week turned into one month, and then three...It was bad enough going to the post office each day...if I'd had to deal with her phone calls on top of everything else, I don't know that I could have handled it."

"I wish Colonel Lents would have..."

"Don't blame him. I talked to him, but the more I think about our conversation, I'm convinced he didn't know anything more than I did." She dumped the cooked potatoes into a bowl and then got out the mixer, milk and butter. "He seemed really sorry that he couldn't give me some sort of news."

"I'm sure he was. He told me they didn't even keep him in on the loop. He definitely didn't know we'd been captured." He paused and then asked, "Can we talk about something else? I've spent the last few days telling and re-telling everything that happened over there, and right now I'd just like to forget about it for a while."

Maddie nodded and then started up the mixer, the noise making further conversation pointless for the moment. Jeff grinned at her and she grinned back. "Very nice. I'll have to add a mixer to my bag of tricks so the next time the shrinks come after me, I can just avoid their questions because of the noise."

Maddie chuckled, "I don't think the military is going to like seeing their big strong soldiers walking around with small kitchen appliances attached to their belts."

Jeff paused for a moment as the image took shape in his mind and then he laughed for the first time in months. He could just see his team members with mixers, can openers, blenders hanging off of their gear belts. It felt so good to laugh, he couldn't resist keeping the joke going a few seconds longer, "Hey, if we made those part of the essential mission gear, we could always stop and whip up a cake or even an omelet…gear that serves more than one purpose always gets my vote."

Maddie looked at him for a moment and then burst into giggles, "I can almost see the recruitment posters now. Big muscled guys with their camo pants, AK-47s strapped across their chests, and a mixer and an oven mitt held in their hands."

Jeff shook his head, "I happen to know that most of the guys on my team can't cook anything that doesn't come in a foil packet…that type of gear would be completely wasted on them."

Maddie nodded her head, her giggles continuing as she removed the chicken from the pan of oil and set it on some paper towels to drain. She lifted two plates down from the cabinet and began dishing food up, taking only half as much as she dished up for him and prompting him to give a half-hearted protest.

"Are you trying to fatten me up?" he teased her as she slid the plates across the counter.

Maddie eyed him critically. "You've lost weight. Quite a bit, if I'm not mistaken."

Jeff sobered at the reminder of where he'd been the last few months. "Providing nutritious meals wasn't exactly high on the priority list of my hosts."

Maddie slid onto a bar stool and then sobered as well, "It was bad, wasn't it?" She searched his eyes, reading the answer there before he gave her a brisk nod and then dug into his food. Jeff was much relieved when she took the hint and began eating as well.

He helped her clean up the dishes, insisting that since she cooked, he would clean up, but she insisted on helping him, saying it would make the task much faster. After shutting off the kitchen lights, they adjourned to her living room where she handed him the remote control and excused herself for a few minutes.

Jeff hadn't watched much television in the time since he'd been rescued, and he found himself lazily searching through the satellite channels, not really interested in anything he was seeing. He kept an ear open for Maddie's return, but after twenty minutes and no sign of her, he turned the television off and wandered down the hallway in search of her. She wasn't in the bedroom, although the lamp on the nightstand had been turned on and the bed turned down.

He slipped his shoes off and then wandered around the room for a few minutes, then small sounds coming through the wall captured his attention. He stepped closer, pushing aside the momentary guilt he felt at eavesdropping on his wife's obvious conversation with herself...*or was she talking on the phone to someone? No, definitely not.* He could almost envision her staring at her reflection in the mirror and giving herself the pep talk he currently was listening in on.

Maddie girl, there's nothing to be nervous about. This is Jeff. Your husband. The man you fell madly in love with on your second date. Just because he's been gone for more than half a year doesn't matter. This is what you've been praying for since the day he left. He's back, and you can't let your fear of him leaving again keep you from being the wife you promised him you'd be.

He was the first man you ever really fell in love with and the first man you ever gave both your body and heart to...Take Jess's advice and live one day at a time. You can't know what horrible things he's has to endure these last few months, but you can let him know that you still love him and are so happy he's back.

There was a slight pause and Jeff listened, wondering if she was going to continue, or finally come out of the bathroom. He understood her nervousness, feeling some of the same thing himself. They'd only dated for five weeks before he'd received his deployment orders and he rushed her to the altar.

He'd already asked her to marry him, but rather than taking several months to plan a wedding that would include both of their families, and provide Maddie with the wedding of her dreams, he'd needed to tie her to him before he left the country. It had been a selfish act on his part, but she'd seemed completely onboard with his request, and they'd visited the local magistrate the next morning, saying their vows to one another with no one other than the court clerk as their witness.

Jeff had wanted to keep her all to himself, and it wasn't until they'd gone back to the base three days later that he'd told his team and his CO about his new marital status. Filling out the next of kin paperwork had been hard, but a necessary evil that went with the job he did for Uncle Sam. If something were to happen to him, he wanted to make sure Maddie would be notified and received what little insurance the government thought his life was worth. It was maudlin and not something he'd discussed with her, not wanting to scare her any more than was necessary.

He'd taken a copy of their marriage license to the benefits office, using her personal information contained therein to complete the forms, with her none the wiser. His teammates hadn't been as willing to give him a free pass. When word leaked out that he'd gotten hitched, he'd had everything from warm wishes, to curses and dire warnings about being stupid. Several of the guys on his team had tried marriage, but the demands of their job were hard to bear and none of their wives had stuck around to offer any kind of long-term support.

He was pulled from his meanderings when she started talking to herself again…

Maddie, this is stupid. Get yourself together and go out there and be with your man. He's your husband. He's not exactly a stranger…you remembered what he liked to eat and drink tonight. And his kisses were amazing! Go sit on the couch with him and stop trying to overthink things.

Jeff heard the water turn on and he backed away from the wall, pushing his shoes over to the corner and then heading back for the living room. His little bride was nervous to be alone with him it seemed, and he knew finding out he'd heard her little self-talk would only magnify her embarrassment and nervousness. He settled on the couch just as the bathroom door opened and signaled him she was finally returning.

He turned and watched her walk towards him, seeing that she'd pulled her hair up into a messy ponytail and had changed into fleece pajama pants and a long-sleeved t-shirt that matched her eyes in color. She looked so young and fresh and suddenly, Jeff's nerves got the best of him. Compared to her, he was tainted and battered.

"Sorry it took me so long," she gave him a tentative smile and he didn't miss how she clasped her hands together, her knuckles almost white as she called upon her courage to join him.

He watched her and patted the cushion next to him, "I couldn't seem to settle on any one thing to watch."

Maddie shrugged her shoulders, "I usually just watch a movie…I don't watch much television here and at the clinic, it's usually kid shows. They really like the singing dinosaurs and weird little troll dolls."

Jeff chuckled as she sat down beside him, "I remember watching cartoons on Saturday morning when I was little."

"And when you were older?" she asked with a more relaxed smile.

Jeff inwardly smiled to himself, having decided that he and his bride needed to get to know one another all over again to ease both of their nerves. So far, it seemed to be working. "When I got old enough to ski, we hit the slopes as soon as the lifts started up. In the summertime, we were usually fishing or camping, sometimes hiking in the Canyonlands...there was always some new adventure awaiting us outdoors."

"Your parents went with you?"

Jeff smiled and nodded, "They're the ones who gave me my love for nature." He sobered up and then told her, "I called them before I left Colorado Springs earlier today...to tell them I was okay and such. They'd been worried but they also knew I would call them when I could. My mom is insisting I come to Utah to visit them real soon."

Maddie nodded her head, "They must have been so worried about you."

"Yeah, but this wasn't my first deployment and they knew as long as the black car and uniformed officers didn't show up at their front door, I was still alive and would contact them when I could."

Maddie huffed out a breath, "I tried using that logic but it only got me so far. Before leaving the base, I used to sit facing the apartment window."

"So that you'd be prepared if they came knocking?"

"So that I could see the car when it pulled up and duck out the backdoor. I convinced myself that if I didn't have to hear their words, then I wouldn't have to face the reality that you were gone."

Jeff saw her eyes glisten and pulled her into the shelter of his arms, "Hey, don't start crying again. I'm here and I'm not going anywhere, not for a long while."

Maddie nodded and pushed away from him, "How long is that?"

Jeff cupped her jaw, kissing her forehead and then taking her lips gently with his own, "At least three months."

Three months? She mouthed the words, and then wiped her tears with her fingertips, "Three months is longer than we've actually known one another."

Jeff nodded and gave her an encouraging smile in return, "Yeah, it is." He pulled her back to sit with him on the couch and then picked up the remote control once more. He loved having her in his arms, and as much as he'd love to carry her down the hallway to her bedroom, he also didn't want to do anything that would upset her.

"What kind of movie do you feel like watching?" he asked, flipping through the channels until he came to the upper ones.

"Anything, I don't really care. Just not horror or bad sci-fi," she added as a side note.

Jeff grinned, "No horror or bad sci-fi. Got it. How about this one?" he asked, stopping on a newer comedy about a dysfunctional family that decided the answer to their problems was spending time together on a boat for vacation.

Maddie nodded, "I've heard it's funny, but I haven't had a chance to watch it yet."

Jeff clicked the channel and then tossed the remote to the far side of the couch, "Done. That was fairly easy." He settled back in the cushions, pulling her a little closer into the crook of his arm, loving the way she laid her head on his chest and let her arm wrap around his middle. This was what he'd missed most while being held in captivity – human contact.

Jeff had grown up in a household where his mom routinely hugged him and it wasn't unusual to see his father wrapping his arm around his son's shoulders when he'd been away for a while. One of the things he'd liked most about Maddie was the fact that she was of a similar mindset. She hugged freely and had no problem physically demonstrating her compassion for others. She'd held his hand the first day they'd met, and during the long hours of his confinement, he'd done his best to remember the smell of her shampoo, the feel of her hands on his face, and what it had felt like to wake up in the morning with her snuggled up against him in her peaceful slumber.

Those memories had kept him going and given him something to hold onto, and while he couldn't fathom doing anything else but being in the military, he also couldn't imagine living through another mission like this last one. He had a decision to make, but not for many weeks, and in the meantime, he was going to make as many new memories as possible...just in case.

Chapter 9

Early the next morning...

Maddie heard the knocking on her apartment door and struggled to wake, noticing several things all within seconds of coming back to a semi-awake state. Firstly, she was laying curled around something very warm and hard, and when she curled her fingers they tangled in the soft fabric of a t-shirt. Jeff's t-shirt, to be exact.

Secondly, she was still on the couch, snuggled in his embrace with the television softly playing in front of them. She could see the remote control laying several feet away, on the other side of Jeff's sleeping form, and she immediately gave up the notion of turning it off. She closed her eyes and allowed herself to enjoy being held in her husband's arms once again. The events of yesterday came rushing back and she tried not to let her grief over Annsley's death intrude on the peaceful feeling. Jeff was back and that was what she was going to focus on now.

The knocking on her apartment door came again and she pushed herself out of his arms, rubbing sleep from her eyes as she struggled to figure out what time it was. She finally cleared her blurry eyes and to her amazement saw it was already 7 o'clock in the morning. *Wow!*

She looked over at Jeff to see him slowly coming awake as well, "Good morning." She busied herself to keep from having to meet his eyes, suddenly worried about how messy her hair was and whether or not she had horrible morning breath. She wasn't a vain person, and these types of concerns caught her by surprise.

Jeff sat up and then smoothed a hand over her hair, which had come out of the ponytail band sometime during the night. "What time is it?"

Maddie nodded towards the clock, "It's already 7 and I have to be to work in thirty minutes."

"We must have fallen asleep during the movie," Jeff told her, reaching for the remote control and turning the television off. "Did you get any sleep?"

Maddie nodded, "Yes, I actually feel like I got a lot of sleep."

"You sound surprised by that," Jeff told her, touching her shoulder in order to get her to look at him.

She did so shyly and then nodded, "I haven't really slept well in months. I usually wake up several times a night…" She broke off, not wanting to tell him that for months she'd been having something akin to nightmares about him. They'd started shortly after her move to Castle Peaks and almost always involved Jeff being killed in some horrific way. She'd been so disturbed by them, that she'd sought Pastor Jameson's counsel.

He'd listened to her story and the nightmares and suggested that maybe she should use those times to pray for her husband. Rather than allowing worry to overshadow her existence, she should use those times as reminders to pray for his safe return. Maddie had taken his advice and immediately she'd noticed a difference. Oh, she still had the nightmares…er, rather, she'd been having them up until last night…but as she prayed for Jeff's safety, she could sense peace and comfort coming from above. People who didn't believe in God would probably never understand, but she did and it was the only reason she'd kept sane these last five or so months. Knowing that Jeff had been in desperate need of her prayers during his captivity, now made her wonder if she'd not been awakened for the specific purpose of interceding for him. She made a mental note to seek Pastor Jameson out and ask him about that at her earliest convenience.

Another knock on the door, this time accompanied by Trent's voice coming from the hallway captured her attention once more. "Maddie? Is everything alright in there?"

"Sounds like your fishing partners for the day are here," she told him, finally meeting his eyes and feeling her heart skip a beat at the knowledge that she was married to this handsome man. Jeff was a strong man in both physical body and mind, and she was so happy to have him home she instinctively leaned forward and hugged him tight. She broke away a moment later and looked towards the door, "Can you get the door while I head for the shower?" She pushed off the couch and started for the hallway before he could even answer.

Jeff nodded his head and pushed himself to a standing position, watching her leave before heading to answer the door. He pulled it open to see both Bryan and Trent standing there. "Hey! Come on in, we just woke up."

Bryan and Trent shared a smirk and entered, "Long night?"

Jeff didn't know these men but he felt a kinship with them anyway, and right now, he could use a friend or two in this small town. "Not really. We started watching some movie and must have fallen asleep. I'm not surprised since I'm still on a completely different time zone...I guess all of the emotional upheaval of yesterday wore her out as well."

He wandered back into the living room, "I didn't realize we'd be leaving quite so early. Maddie's trying to get ready for work since she has to be there in thirty minutes."

"No one's going to mind if she's a bit late this morning," Trent assured him. "I'll text Sara and let her know to alert the day shift."

Jeff nodded and then stretched his arms over his head, his t-shirt rising up above the waistband of his jeans. Trent made a noise and Jeff immediately lowered his arms, pulling the t-shirt down at the same time. *Darn it! I forgot about those scars.* He looked up and realized that both Trent and Bryan had seen them and didn't appear ready to ignore their existence. Jeff mentally prepared himself for the questions he could see building in their eyes.

"Looks like you didn't escape your last mission completely unscathed," Bryan told him softly.

Jeff shook his head, and answered shortly, "But I lived. Four of my men can't say that today." He really didn't want to get into this right now. Last night was the first time since being rescued he could remember sleeping through the night and not waking up plagued by nightmares and the accusing faces of the four men he'd lost over there. Damon Powers. Estefan Cerillo. Parker Brubaker. Dmitri Roswell. They'd been members of his team for the last three years and had saved his life more than once. He only wished he'd been able to return the favor this time around.

"That's tough, man," Trent told him, drawing him out of his memories and back to the present.

Jeff shrugged, "As soon as Maddie gets out of the shower, I'll get ready. I don't really have the right kind of gear for this type of adventure."

Trent and Bryan watched him for a moment and then appeared willing to let their questions lie for the time being. Jeff was relieved when everyone shifted their feet and the tension in the room seemed to dissipate. *Thank you, God!*

Trent stepped back towards the hallway and reached for something, bringing it inside with him and then shutting the door once more. He grinned at him and then tossed him the large duffel bag he'd carried in and set by the door. "Everything you need should be in there. Once we get on the ice, there's a rather nice icehouse already set up."

Jeff nodded and unzipped the bag, seeing a variety of warm weather clothing, a pair of water-proof boots, and outerwear. "Thanks."

"What size boots do you wear?" Bryan asked.

"10 ½ or 11," Jeff replied, setting the bag down on the couch and beginning to remove the contents.

"Those should fit just fine then," Bryan told him. He started to say something else, but his cell phone went off and he pulled it from his waist, glancing at the screen and then frowning, "I need to take this call. I'll just step outside for a moment."

Trent gave him a curious look, but then nodded and took a seat on a vacant chair, "Everything go okay last night?"

Jeff sank down onto the couch, listening for the sound of the shower to turn off, "I guess, I didn't really think about how hard coming home would be."

"How's that?" Trent asked, leaning forward with his hands resting between his knees.

Jeff sighed, "Maddie and I were only married for a week before I shipped out…"

"What? A week? Man, that's tough." Trent was quiet and then he looked at Jeff, "How long did you two know each other before you got married?"

Jeff looked at him and then shook his head with a halfhearted laugh, "Five weeks. She was like finding my other half, as corny as that may sound."

Trent shook his head, "Not at all. The first time I met Sara, I knew almost immediately that she was different. We only knew each other a few days before I realized she was the girl of my dreams and the one I wanted to spend the rest of my life with."

Jeff nodded, "That's how it was for us, but we planned on taking our time. I thought maybe I'd have a few months on base before getting deployed, but we only had a few weeks. We got married by the local judge and didn't even have time to tell either of our parents. None of them know we're married even today."

"I've been gone for almost nine months…it kind of feels like we're strangers, but I love her. She was what kept me going when I was over there…I still believe we were meant to be together, but I can sense she's nervous and is wondering when I'll have to leave again. I hate the fear I can see lurking in her eyes."

Trent said nothing for a moment and then asked, "Is leaving again a possibility?"

Jeff shook his head, "I have at least three months… maybe more. I have to make some tough decisions, and right now, the thought of going on mission again really scares me. I've never felt that way before and it has me wondering if I can do this job anymore. Things were so bad over there…I just don't know…"

Bryan had come back in, hearing his last comments, and now he sat down and asked, "Did you talk to anyone when you got back?"

Jeff knew what he was asking and then he nodded, "Yeah, several shrinks. I heard all of the usual advice about not feeling guilty and jumping back into my life as a way to honor the lives that were lost…I'm sure they all meant well, but they weren't there. I was, and the four men who were killed were part of my team and I considered them my family. They didn't deserve what happened to them." *Especially since they were killed and tortured because of me.*

"I know about those kinds of losses and all I can tell you is that it gets better with time. You have to examine the situation and decide if there was anything you could have done to change the outcome. If the answer is no, you have to let the guilt go and move on with your life or it will eat you up just like a cancer. It's hard and will take some work, but just take each day on its own and it will get better." Bryan knew more than a little about this, having been in deep cover for so many months and having to watch innocent victims fall in order to continue his cover and ultimately take down the entire cartel. Their deaths still haunted him at times, but he was learning to live despite them.

A noise behind Jeff had him turning to see Maddie standing in the hallway, wrapped in a fluffy pink robe, and watching him with unshed tears sparkling in her eyes. Jeff surged to his feet, "Maddie..."

She shook her head and came towards him, wrapping her arms around him and squeezing him tight, "I'm so sorry you had to go through that. I know you don't want to talk about it right now, but when you do, I want you to know I'll be here to listen."

Jeff was shocked at her words and then realized she'd been standing in the hallway for more than just a few seconds. He wrapped his arms around her and took strength from her embrace, so grateful to have her still in his life. He knew many women would have given up on waiting for their new husband to return and would have sought a divorce or annulment. Maddie hadn't done either, and for that he would be eternally grateful.

"So, why don't you go get ready to go fishing so we can get out of here?" Trent suggested after several minutes.

Maddie pulled away from Jeff and blushed when he kissed her briefly on the lips, he grinned at the other men, "It won't take me long."

Maddie watched him go and then excused herself to dress for the day. As she headed down the hallway, Trent called out after her,

"I sent Sara a message telling her you were going to be late so take your time getting ready."

She waved at him from the bedroom door, "Thanks. I shouldn't be more than a few minutes late."

"I'll let her know. You look happy," he commented.

Maddie thought for a minute and then smiled, "I am. Like Annsley said, my waiting is over."

Chapter 10

Six hours later...

Maddie parked in the church parking lot and then got out and started up the concrete path to the chapel portion of the building. Things had been very slow at the clinic, and after an emotional goodbye with Annsley's parents, Sara had sent all non-essential personnel home. There were four nurses scheduled for the day shift, but only two were needed, so Maddie and their newest hire, Alaina Drake, were sent home for the rest of the day.

Alaina was the youngest nurse on staff, having just finished her nursing degree in December and having only been at the clinic for three weeks thus far. She was a quiet girl and tended to keep to herself, but she was very competent in her job and the kids seemed to like her gentle spirit. Maddie had been so caught up in everything else, she'd not taken time to get to know the new girl very well, but as she had watched her drive away from the clinic, she made a vow to change that in the coming days and weeks.

For herself, she had decided to seek out Pastor Jameson's counsel sooner, rather than later. She stepped into the chapel, expecting to see the Pastor, but instead she found Grace sitting on the front pew, her eyes red and puffy from crying.

"Grace?" Maddie whispered, coming to sit down beside her.

Grace lifted her head and then tried to wipe her tears away, "Oh, hey. What are you doing here?" She looked around to see if Maddie was all alone. Her shoulder drooped when she saw no one else and Maddie was sure she'd not seen her look any more tired than she did now.

"Is everything alright? When we spoke yesterday, I thought Dr. Mike was coming back to Castle Peaks today."

Grace nodded, "He is, later this afternoon. We're heading home tomorrow."

Maddie nodded and then asked, "Are you crying about what happened yesterday? She'd been so immersed in her own grief, she now felt guilty for not thinking about how Grace might have taken the little girl's death.

Grace shook her head, "No, I cried for her yesterday."

Maddie nodded, "Then do you mind me asking what has you in tears today?"

Grace clasped her hands together and started to worry her fingers together. "I didn't realize anyone else would be here at this time of day. Pastor Jameson is at the clinic and didn't expect to be back for a while."

"So, you came here to be alone and cry?" Maddie asked, sensing something was really bothering this woman. She'd only met her a few times, but none of those had shown Grace to be a weak woman.

Grace looked at her and then burst into tears again, "I can't do this."

Maddie was confused and laid a gentle hand on her shoulder, "Can't do what? Is this about your pregnancy?"

Grace nodded and Maddie was even more confused. Grace had seemed so happy about things the day before, seeing her tears now was shocking. "I thought you were happy about having another baby?"

Grace tried to smile through her tears, "I am. I really am, but…"

"But what?" Maddie asked quietly.

Grace took several deep breaths and calmed herself, blanking her expression and doing her best to shut off her emotions. Maddie watched the change come over her and was alarmed by it. "Grace, what's going on?"

"I think...I think I have cancer," she said the words in a whisper and fresh tears leaked from her eyes.

"What?" Maddie exclaimed. "Why would you think that?" she asked, trying to play the calm and collected nurse. "Have you told your husband or talked to a doctor?"

Grace shook her head, "No. I just found...a lump...under my arm...this morning. This can't be happening. I watched my mother die of cancer and I know what Tori went through...I'm pregnant...why is this happening now?"

Maddie scooted closer and wrapped the other woman in a hug, "Maybe this isn't what you think it is? Just because your mom had cancer doesn't mean anything..."

Grace pushed away and shook her head, "But it does mean my risk is higher. I've wanted another child, one with Mike, for months, and now that I'm finally pregnant, this happens? I don't know what to do!"

Maddie shook her head and put on her best stern nurse face, "I'll tell you what you're going to do. You're going to talk to your husband and go see a doctor if he doesn't want to check things out. Until you know for sure what you're dealing with, you're worrying and putting the baby at risk for nothing."

Grace kept crying and Maddie reached for a box of tissues, handing her several and waiting while she tried to pull herself together. "I can't...what if..."

"Stop imaging the worst. When's your husband due back?" Maddie asked, pushing aside her own needs for the woman sitting next to her.

Grace looked at her watch and then gave her a watery smile, "He's probably at Trent and Sara's right now."

"Do you want me to drive you over there? I really think you should go talk to him..."

"Grace? Sweetheart, what are you...," Michael Simpson asked as he walked down the aisle of the church. Neither woman had heard the outer doors open and he was looking between them as if he couldn't quite decide who was having the problem.

Grace stood up and then stumbled from the pews and into his arms, sobbing brokenly.

Michael looked at Maddie and she simply shook her head and excused herself, "I'll leave you two alone." As she passed by them, she whispered to him, "Make her talk to you. Today." She knew there was an urgency in her voice that he would pick up on, but it couldn't be helped. If Grace had found a lump in the lymph nodes under her arm, there was definite cause for alarm, and Maddie was the first one to advise having a professional evaluate the potential problem.

She exited the church, hoping everything with Grace was going to work out and that she was alarmed for no reason, but she dealt with cancer every day and when it came to the dreadful disease and its various forms and disguises, she wasn't willing to take any chances. The tiniest spot or lump deserved to be examined and treated early, if indeed it was found to be malignant. That was the best course of action and gave the patient the best chance for survival and beating the horrid disease.

She headed for her vehicle, just as Jeff and Pastor Jameson arrived in separate cars. She was surprised to see Jeff back so soon and waited patiently while they both got out of their vehicles and joined her on the sidewalk.

"Hey! I thought you would still be fishing with Trent and Bryan," she told Jeff, accepting his hug and the kiss on her forehead while Pastor Jameson looked on.

"Bryan got an urgent phone call about an hour ago and needed to come back to town right away."

"Is everything alright?" she asked, wondering what was going on with him. "Was there an accident up on the highway?"

Jeff shook his head, "No, this has something to do with his new business. Trent stopped in at the station and everything is fine."

Maddie looked at Pastor Jameson, "I came by to see you for a few minutes, but since Jeff's back, maybe we can talk later in the week." It wasn't what she'd planned for, but in light of Grace and Michael's current distress, her problems and questions seemed minor at the moment. "Grace was here when I arrived and she's really upset. Michael is inside with her now."

Pastor Jameson looked towards the chapel and nodded, "I'll go see if I can be of assistance. Jeff, it was a pleasure to meet you and I welcome any help you want to give me."

"Sure thing, Pastor. How about I come by sometime tomorrow and you can show me those plans?"

Pastor Jameson nodded, "That sounds good. Have a nice afternoon and evening, both of you."

"Bye, Pastor." Maddie watched him enter the chapel and then turned to her husband, "What plans?"

"The little girl who died...her parents made a donation to the clinic and town to build a memorial garden in her honor. The church

79

already has plans for a solarium to be built in the courtyard and Sara and Mr. Mercer suggested the funds be combined with what the church has already raised to build the solarium here.

"I worked in a greenhouse during the summer months while I was growing up and offered to help with some plant selections and that quickly escalated to where I think I've now been put in charge of seeing this project gets going."

Maddie smiled at his confused look, "Welcome to Castle Peaks. Everyone here is really nice, but they don't really know the meaning of the word 'No' and everyone gets roped into helping on these types of projects. You'll have plenty of help from the men of the town, and when it comes to planting, probably more help from the women than you could ever imagine or want."

Jeff grinned, "Well, if I remember correctly, work parties are where you gain the most knowledge about everyone else. My mom used to say there was no better place to hear gossip than at the beauty salon or a church bazaar. I'm guessing a church work party is much the same way."

"I've only been here a few months, but that would be about right from what I've observed."

"Good to know. So, is everything else okay? You were coming to see Pastor Jameson?"

Maddie nodded, "I've talked to him a couple of times since moving here." She didn't elaborate on the topic they'd discussed and she found herself wondering what Jeff's response would be if she were to tell him. *Would he be upset that she'd discussed her marriage with someone else? And if she told him about the nightmares, what would he say then? Would he think she was a little bit crazy? That was what she'd thought about herself initially, and only after talking with the kind Pastor had she been able to step outside of herself and see them for what they could be...a sign from above that Jeff needed help.*

A gust of cold air brought her back to the fact that they were both standing outside in the cold, and that the sun was going down already and the temperature was dropping fast. "We should probably get out of this weather." Dark clouds had rolled over the mountains earlier that afternoon and Maddie was almost certain they were in for another snowstorm.

"That sounds good. I saw a grocery store in town...how about I stop by there and pick up a couple of steaks for that grill on your deck?"

Maddie smiled, "It's too cold to grill outside."

"Says who?" Jeff asked with an answering grin.

"Well...no one, I guess. I've never tried it."

Jeff only grinned more, "I grew up where we had lots of snow, believe me, it can be done and there's something about a grilled steak...I haven't had anything that good since the night before I left."

Maddie nodded and bit her bottom lip, remembering well the night before he'd deployed. They'd eaten in, steaks, baked potatoes, and fresh bread from the local bakery. Even though it hadn't been cold outside, Jeff had lit a fire in the small fireplace in their apartment and they'd eaten their dinner on a large blanket spread out in front of the fire.

Maddie had lit candles around the room giving everything a very intimate and secluded feel, and they'd spent the night there, talking about their dreams and hopes for the future and loving one another. It had been a magical night, even more so than their wedding night in her mind, and for the first few months he'd been gone, she'd relived those moments as a way to hold onto him.

Thinking about them now, after pushing them aside for months, she yearned to recapture that with her husband. A man she needed to get to know all over again. She wanted to share her hopes and dreams with him once again, and she had a feeling that if she were to ask anyone for advice, they would tell her to stop being fearful and reach for what she wanted.

Jeff was watching her carefully and she realized he was hoping for an answer. She smiled at him and then nodded, "Steaks sound good. I've got some potatoes at the apartment I can start as soon as I get home."

Jeff gave her a relieved smile and then stepped closer to her, cupping the back of her neck with one hand and using the other to gently touch her bottom lip, "Tell me I'm not pushing too fast here."

Maddie swallowed and then told him what she was feeling, "I don't know if I can, but I don't want to feel nervous around you...I want what we had before."

"So do I, sweetheart. So do I." Jeff kissed her gently on the lips and then backed away when he realized she was now shivering in the cold. "Go home and I'll be there in a bit."

Maddie nodded and headed for her vehicle, slipping inside and then watching as he did the same. She felt excited and hopeful about this evening and she hurried home, pulling candles from drawers and making sure everything was as perfect as could be before he got back. Tonight, she wanted to live out the fantasy of greeting her husband on his return from battle. She'd envisioned his homecoming for weeks and months, but yesterday had taken her by surprise and circumstances had placed a damper on things. That wasn't going to happen tonight. She didn't have to work for another two days and she was going to take advantage of that fact and get to know about her husband all over again.

Chapter 11

Two days later...

Jeff was falling in love with Castle Peaks and the people who lived there. He'd spent the day before with his lovely wife, and for the first time since seeing her again, he felt like they really were truly married. Two nights earlier, they'd re-created their last night together before his deployment, and it had ended up with the two of them reaffirming their love for one another and sleeping in the same bed. Jeff knew they would still have things to work through, but he was definitely encouraged that they were on the same page for now.

Maddie and he had been planning to go cross country skiing today, but this morning she'd gotten a phone call from Sara asking if she would mind watching the kids for a few hours. It seemed that her sister Grace and her husband hadn't returned to San Diego the day before, as planned, because Grace wasn't feeling well and Michael had insisted on running some tests on her. Maddie had been overly concerned with Grace's health and she'd been more than a little agitated until Jeff had told her they could go skiing another time.

Maddie had hurried over to Sara's home to watch her children and Grace's daughter Daniella, and Jeff had headed into town to join Trent and Bryan for lunch at the diner. That was where he currently sat, listening to people as they came and went, trying to remember names and the like as everyone introduced themselves. He didn't consider himself good with names and knew he would never come close to remembering half of the people's names the next time they met on the street.

"I know it's a lot to take in," Bryan told him, "but you'll get used to it. I did and I really didn't like socializing much when I came here."

"I don't have a problem with socializing, but remembering all of those names and who goes with who...that's going to take more than a cursory introduction."

"It'll come, just give it time. Tomorrow's Sunday, do you plan on attending church with Maddie?" Trent asked as the waitress brought their lunch over.

"She hasn't said anything about it, but we attended church together in the Springs, so I don't see why that won't happen here."

"Good, that will help you remember people as well. I heard you were going to take on the solarium project...coming tomorrow will give you a chance to meet some of the others who will want to have a hand in helping."

"Great," Jeff told him. "I'm actually quite thankful to have something to do with my time. Downtime isn't something I'm used to."

"Didn't you have downtime at the base between missions?" Bryan asked, taking a bite of his sandwich.

Jeff nodded, "Yes and no. We had downtime, but then we usually filled it up with giving the trainers a break."

"You worked with the new recruits?" Trent asked.

"Some. That's actually how I met Maddie. I got cut by some barbed wire and had to go in for stitches. She was working in the base hospital and one thing led to another. Five weeks later I got my mission papers and we got married the next day." A stab of guilt over the fact that neither of their parents had been told about their children's married state entered his brain.

"So, neither of you have told your parents?" Trent asked in amazement.

Jeff shook his head, "No, we discussed calling them both yesterday, but we decided we probably needed to tell them in person, and preferably together." Jeff paused and then asked, "I was thinking that maybe we needed to have another wedding ceremony... invite our parents and have a real church wedding...I know that was Maddie's dream and she pushed that aside because of the timing..."

Trent grinned at him, "I don't know you or Maddie all that well, but I know my Sara, and she'd be thrilled with something like that. In fact, I think we could easily ask Sara and Jess to handle the details and such."

Bryan grinned, "And if you play your cards right and get married three weeks from now, Trent's cousin will be here with her husband and she could do the cooking. Trust me, she's worth waiting for."

Things were moving too fast and Jeff held up a hand, "Guys, I appreciate the support but it was just a suggestion..."

"Why not make it a reality? You said you thought Maddie was acting nervous and such...give her the wedding of her dreams."

Jeff thought about how happy something like that might make Maddie, but there were so many logistical problems to be handled. Her parents. His parents. He'd want his teammates there, if possible. There was decorating. Invitation. A cake. Flowers. The list was staggering already, and he knew there were probably dozens of things he'd not even thought about yet.

He looked up and Trent and Bryan were grinning at him, "Leave it to us and the rest of the town. We haven't had anything exciting to get behind since Christmas."

"Let me talk to Maddie..."

"Absolutely not! No, make this all a big surprise for her."

"How do you keep the need for a wedding dress a surprise?" Jeff asked, liking where this idea was headed, but completely at odds with how to make it happen.

Trent smiled, "Leave it to me. I'll put it in Sara's capable hands and I'm sure she'll come up with something. Besides, it will give her and Grace something to focus on besides what they don't know."

Jeff sobered and asked, "Maddie said there was a potential problem with Grace?"

"She just found out she's pregnant again. She'd not even told Michael, her husband, yet and then she found a lump under her arm. Grace and Sara's mom died of cancer and Grace has had several friends go through breast cancer. She automatically thought the worst, but because of the pregnancy, they can't even do some of the testing for another few weeks. The first trimester is tricky when it comes to anesthesia and x-rays…they'll need to monitor her closely and wait until after she's twelve weeks before they can do the needed scans and take a biopsy."

"Wow! That's rough. No wonder Maddie was so upset. Grace must be really scared."

"She is, but she's also strong and can handle this, she just needs to focus on other things. They did some bloodwork today and that should give them some sort of indication if there's really something wrong or just a minor disturbance."

"Well, I'll pray for a good outcome."

"Prayers work," Pastor Jameson announced as he stopped by the table, having heard Jeff's last comment.

"Pastor, good to see you," Trent and Bryan both greeted the man.

"Pastor, I'll be by the church Monday morning to take a look at those plans."

"Fine, fine. I didn't mean to interrupt your lunch, but I hear people talking about prayers and find I can't keep quiet."

"We were discussing Grace," Trent informed him.

"Ah! Well, she definitely needs our prayers and God's peace. Many people don't believe in the power of prayer, you know?" He looked at Jeff, "Your wife, for instance. She came to me months ago and I believe she would be the first to verify that prayers do have a positive effect upon us."

"Maddie came to you about praying?" Jeff asked, confused because Maddie, like himself, had been raised in a good Christian home and praying together hadn't been a foreign concept to either of them.

"She couldn't seem to get rid of the nightmares and I suggested she pray when they came, rather than allowing fear to rule the night."

"Good advice, Pastor," Trent told him.

"Yes, well it seemed to do the trick. Anyway, I'll look forward to seeing you tomorrow, gentlemen. Have a good day."

Jeff continued to let the conversation about the wedding circulate between Trent and Bryan, nodding and answering when prodded, but his mind was fixated on something the Pastor had said. It seemed that his little bride hadn't been completely honest with him about how she'd handled his absence. She'd led him to believe that she'd been strong and had steered clear of excessive worry and depression over his lengthy absence. *Nightmares? That didn't seem to fit the picture she'd painted.*

Jeff headed home a few hours later, intending to see if he could get Maddie to open up to him about her nightmares. The only thing that kept him hesitant, was the niggling little voice inside his head that told him he would also need to be prepared to share his own nightmares with her if they were to truly open up to one another.

Maybe we're not quite there yet. She doesn't need to know everything I dream about at night. That would surely send her running in the opposite direction. No, better to just let things alone and at some point, in the future, they can confess their fears and anxieties to one another. Right now, he was focused on dreams and hopes. That was where they future lie, not in dredging up the past.

Chapter 12

February 19th, Sunday afternoon...

Maddie listened to Pastor Jameson's sermon, very aware of the man sitting by her side. Most of the townsfolk now knew she was married and that her husband had miraculously returned from a military operation, but many of them hadn't met him yet. Based upon the looks they received when they'd arrived at the church an hour earlier, they intended to correct that error as soon as possible.

"Nice sermon," Jeff told her as the final benediction was given and people stood up in preparation for leaving. He picked up her coat and held it for her while she slipped her arms inside, turning her around and buttoning it up for her as well.

"Thanks," Maddie told him quietly, sticking her hands into her pockets to feel for her gloves. The most recent storm had dropped half a dozen inches of snow in the last forty-eight hours and today the sky was blue and the sun was shining, but the temperature was barely above freezing and Maddie was wishing for the start of spring.

Finding her gloves, she held them in one hand and then exited the pew in front of Jeff, loving how he once again placed his hand upon her lower back as they exited the building. He'd done that almost from the time they'd first met and the only time he didn't walk with her that way, was when he was holding her hand in his own. Both actions always made her feel safe and cared for and it was one of the many things she'd missed while he'd been gone.

They waited their turn to speak with Pastor Jameson and several people took advantage of their momentary stillness to introduce themselves to Jeff and find out a little bit about him. Bill Mercer was standing directly behind them in the exit line, and after several of the ladies in town, known for the predilection to gossip, waltzed off, he leaned forward and spoke in their ears.

"Take my advice and don't be too free with the information you share with those three. They aren't known for their discretion and they are terrible about assuming the worst."

Maddie turned and looked at him, "Thanks for the head's up, sir. This is my husband, Jeff Young. He just returned from a military operation."

"Well now, I had heard our Maddie was married and wisely chose to keep you hidden until you could put in a personal appearance. Bravo, young lady. Those three troublemakers are a little bent out of shape that they didn't have a chance to spread the news first."

Maddie smiled, "They seem harmless enough."

Bill chuckled and shook his head, "Only if you're already married. They consider themselves matchmakers and I must say they're pretty horrible at it. The last couple they tried to get together ended up hating one another. They didn't stop to find out what kind of work the young people did. He was working for a natural resource exploration company, and she worked for one of them environmental activist groups. Their non-romance was doomed from the beginning."

Jeff couldn't hold back his chuckle, "Bet there were some fireworks when they tried to communicate with one another?"

"Oh, boy! Now, this all happened in the next town over, but that didn't stop those three. No, siree. They met that young man on one of their monthly shopping sprees and immediately set about finding him a nice young wife. They're still looking."

"Glad I'm already married," Maddie told him, smiling at him as they moved forward and came to stand in front of Pastor Jameson.

"Maddie and Jeff. I'm so glad you came this morning," the Pastor told them, shaking both of their hands.

"It was nice to be in church again, Pastor. Especially with my wife beside me. I'll be by tomorrow morning, if that's alright?"

Pastor Jameson nodded, "That's fine. I need to do some visitation in the afternoon, but I'll be around first thing in the morning."

"I'll be here bright and early." Jeff saw Trent and Bryan waving to him and he excused himself, "I'm going to go say hello to a few other people. Meet you at the car?"

Maddie nodded and watched him walk away, pleased that he was making some friends here. This had become her home and the more she thought about leaving and returning to Colorado Springs with Jeff, the more her heart hurt.

"Why are you looking so sad?" Pastor Jameson wanted to know. "I thought things were going well with your husband's return."

"They are, I guess I'm just worrying about the future. He only has three months off and then he and his team could be deployed again. I honestly don't know if I can go through another separation like the last one."

Pastor Jameson patted her shoulder, "Just remember that everything happens for a reason. God knows what we can and cannot bear and he promised to never give us more than we could handle. Of course, he does expect us to come to him for help, but even then, I believe everything we go through has a purpose."

Maddie nodded, "Thanks for the reminder. I probably needed to hear that."

"That's what I'm here for. I hope I didn't overstep myself yesterday when I spoke with Jeff."

Maddie looked perplexed, "You spoke with Jeff yesterday?"

"I ran into him during lunch at the diner. He, Trent and Bryan were discussing Grace's recent scare and I overheard him mention that he would be praying for her. I told him that he had no better example of how well prayer can work than you in regards to your nightmares."

Maddie's eyes opened wide and she glanced at Jeff, alarm making her heartbeat speed up. "Uhm…he didn't say anything to me last night."

"Very good, I was afraid, after I got to thinking about things, that you two might not have gotten to the point of sharing things like that yet. I'm glad to see I was wrong."

"No, everything's good. Thanks again, Pastor. I'll see you later this week." Maddie made her way to the vehicle, her mind spinning circles regarding the Pastor's confession.

If he mentioned my nightmares to Jeff, why didn't he ask me about them last night while we were talking? Does he not care that I was having them? Or does he not want to be bothered with those kinds of things? What happens if I have another one and wake up crying and screaming? Is that going to send him back to the base?

She was sitting in the vehicle, still pondering the answers to her questions when Jeff joined her, "Ready to go home?" he asked in a jovial voice.

Maddie nodded, "Sure." The joy of the day had somewhat waned in light of the fact that she was now worried about the nightmares. She was quiet all the way home, and just before they arrived she could feel Jeff watching her. She looked at him, "Is something wrong?"

Jeff paused for a moment and then answered, "You tell me. You were smiling and seemed happy before I left you to talk to Trent and Bryan. Did Pastor Jameson say something to upset you?"

Maddie shook her head, "I'm not upset."

Jeff raised a brow, but didn't argue with her, "Okay, if you're not upset, then what's bothering you? What did you and Pastor Jameson talk about?"

Maddie shook her head, "Nothing. I'm fine, just tired. Maybe I'm coming down with a cold." She knew she was prevaricating, but that didn't seem to matter in the moment. She did not want to get into her nightmares with Jeff, especially not while they were in the car. If they were going to have that deep of a discussion, it needed to be at the right time and in the right place. This was neither.

Jeff stared at her a moment later and then shook his head and turned into the parking lot for her apartment complex. The fourplexes were fairly new, built just in the last few years to accommodate the workers at the clinic and in the town. Maddie had fallen in love with the modern appliances and special touches that had been added to make them seem more spacious and appealing.

She didn't wait for Jeff to come around and open her door, she simply got out and headed up the stairs. Jeff followed her and she could tell as he entered the apartment behind her that he was confused about her change in attitude. "I'm going to change clothes before I fix us some lunch. Is canned soup and a sandwich okay?"

"Whatever you want to fix is fine with me," he told her, following her down the hallway and stopping at the bedroom door. "Will you please tell me what's changed since I left you speaking with the Pastor?"

Maddie looked at him and then sank down on the mattress of the bed, "I really don't want to have this discussion right now."

Jeff slowly came into the room, squatting down to look her in the eye, "When would you like to have it? Whatever it is has obviously upset you, and if it's something I've done I'd like to know about it."

"It's not something you did, it's something you were told." Maddie looked at him and Jeff quickly went through his activities of the last few days, wondering what she was talking about. The conversation with Pastor Jameson in the diner the day before came rushing back to him and he suddenly knew she was talking about her nightmares.

Jeff took a deep breath and then let it out, "Maddie, Pastor Jameson mentioned that you'd sought his counsel about some nightmares you'd been having and he advised you to pray about them. He didn't tell me what they were about, and I didn't bring it up last night because we've been getting along so well. I didn't want anything negative to spoil what we had going."

Maddie listened to him and then nodded, "I'm probably just overreacting. I haven't said anything about them, probably for some of the same reasons you haven't talked about your captivity. I don't like to dwell on negative things, or things that scare me...I'd rather be at peace and enjoy life."

"Wouldn't we all?" Jeff asked, coming up to a standing position and then sitting down next to her on the mattress. "Look, I haven't said anything about my time over there because I'm not sure I can right now. I don't want to relive those months and right now, they're too fresh. You don't have to tell me about your nightmares until you're ready to do so. Are you still having them?"

Maddie shook her head, "I haven't had any since you got here."

Jeff slipped an arm around her shoulders, "Good, that's real good. I haven't had any nightmares for a while either. That must mean we're good for one another, you think?"

Maddie smiled and then nodded, "I know so."

"Are we good now?" Jeff wanted to know, seeing the smile back on her face and in her eyes.

Maddie nodded, "Let me change and I'll get lunch fixed."

"You got it. Oh, I almost forgot to mention it. Trent invited us over to their house this evening to watch the big game. I told him I thought we could make it. Was that okay?"

Maddie smiled, "Football's biggest game of the season? Yeah, I think we can make it. I'll give Sara a call in a little bit and see what we can bring. It will be fun to spend some time with other people."

Jeff kissed her on the forehead and then pushed up from the mattress, "Great! I'll go start the sandwiches. See you in a few minutes."

Maddie watched him go, relieved that she wasn't going to have to discuss the nightmares right now, or anytime in the near future for that matter. They were gone now, and that was how she liked it. The future was filled with happiness and hope, and she was determined to not let the worries of the past mess that up.

Chapter 13

February 28th, Tuesday, a week and a half before the surprise wedding...

Jeff patiently said goodbye to Maddie as she left for work, watching her vehicle pull away from the apartment complex before he finally breathed a sigh of relief. She thought he was heading to the church to work on the new solarium that was being built and would be dedicated in memory of Annsley, and he would. But later, after he took care of a couple of pressing matters.

Things were already underway as far as the surprise wedding went, but the biggest hurdle was yet to be overcome. Telling their respective parents. Jeff wasn't all that worried about telling his own family, although he recognized there would be some hurt feelings and recriminations that he'd allowed his wife to worry about him all on her own. He was prepared for that, and he knew that no matter what, his parents would still give them their full support. That was just the type of loving people they were.

Speaking with Maddie's parents was an entirely different thing. He'd heard her talk about them and he knew they were slightly older, her father getting ready to retire soon from the railroad he'd worked for most of his adult life. He tried to put himself in their position and acknowledged that he would be very upset if some young man called him one day to tell him he'd married their daughter almost a year earlier, and they were just hearing about it.

Maddie loved her parents and had kept in touch with them during his absence. She'd even told them about her move to Castle Peaks, she just hadn't told them why or the fact that she'd legally changed her last name. She'd explained that her parents would want to meet the man who'd stolen her heart, and since he wasn't around and she couldn't give them a time frame when that might change, it was easier to just put that task off until something changed.

Well, things were changing and quickly. There was no time to waste as both sets of parents needed to be in Castle Peaks a week from this coming Friday, as the wedding was set for Saturday. He sat down on the couch and pulled his cell phone out, dialing his parents' number and hoping that his father would pick up first. He'd always been the more level-headed of his two parents, and he would much rather have his father paving the way for him than taking his chances with not saying the wrong thing and making his mother cry. He hated when she cried because of something he'd done.

He put the phone on speaker and waited for someone to answer.

"Hello?"

"Dad? Hey, it's Jeff."

"Son, it's good to hear from you. Your mother was just telling me she needed to call you. When are you coming home for a visit?"

"I'm not real sure right now. Is mom there?" Jeff asked, thinking maybe he should get both of his parents on the phone at the same time so he only had to tell them once.

"She is. We're heading up to Alta this morning to get some fresh powder skiing in."

"That sounds exciting. Do you have a few minutes to talk before you head out?" Jeff asked, not wanting to delay their excursion, and knowing that he was hoping his dad said no so he could put this conversation off.

"The lifts don't open midweek until 10 o'clock so we have a few hours. Let me get her for you."

"Hey, I was thinking maybe you could put her on the other line, or maybe the speakerphone. That way I can talk to you both at the same time?"

"Now that's something we haven't done in a good long while. Hold on a second."

Jeff heard his father put the phone down and holler for his mother to come into the kitchen. His father had already activated the speakerphone and he smiled at their interaction.

"What are you yelling about in here?" Faith Young's voice echoed through the phone.

"Jeff's on the phone and wants to speak to both of us," he dad replied.

"Really? Oh, you don't think he found a girl, do you? That would be so neat."

Hold that thought, mom. Don't kill the messenger just because I'm a few months late.

"Jeff? Honey, is that you?"

"I'm here, mom. It's good to hear your voice."

"Oh, you too. Your dad said you wanted to talk to both of us?"

"Yes." Jeff paused for effect and then asked, "What are you two doing next weekend?"

"Next weekend?" his mother echoed. "Well, I don't know that we have any kind of plans. Are you planning on coming home...?"

"Not exactly. I was thinking maybe you two could take a trip to Montana."

"Montana?" his father asked. "Son, are you in Montana?"

WAITING FOR LOVE'S RETURN

"Yes, I am."

"But I thought you were stationed in Colorado Springs? Do they even have a base in Montana?" his mother questioned, trying to figure out what he wasn't telling them yet.

"Well, they have a reserve base and a few smaller stations, but nothing I would ever be based out of. No, I'm up here for an entirely different reason."

"So, you're going back to Colorado Springs?" his father asked, for clarification.

"I haven't decided that yet and really, I'd rather talk about this topic when I see you. In Montana. Next Friday. Oh, and mom, you might want to get a new dress, and dad, you can dig out that tuxedo jacket you bought for that cruise a few years ago. This would be the perfect occasion to wear it."

"Oh! Jeff, does this mean...well, I don't want to jump the gun, but it kind of sounds like you're inviting us to ...a wedding?"

"Yes, I am. My wedding."

Just as he knew would happen, his mother burst into tears and he could hear his father trying to calm her down quietly. After a long pause, his father spoke again, "Son, we're so happy for you. Tell us all about her. What's her name? Where did you meet her?"

"Well, that's kind of the other thing I wanted to talk to you about. Now, I know you're going to be upset, but I really would like you to listen to my explanation and try to understand things from my perspective."

"Jeff, you're starting to scare me. What's wrong?"

"Absolutely nothing. In fact, everything's just about perfect. Or, it will be after next Saturday. That's when I getting remarried."

"Remarried?" his father asked. "Son, I do believe your mother and I have missed something. Exactly when did you get married before?"

"A few days before I deployed last time. Maddie and I had been planning to wait and make trips to Georgia and Utah to meet everyone, but then I got my assignment papers months earlier than I expected them to arrive, and we didn't want to wait. We got married in the courthouse in Colorado Springs, and a few days later I shipped out.

"I never expected a two-month mission would turn out like it did, and I certainly never thought I'd leave behind a new bride with no way to contact her."

"Oh, Jeff! Why didn't you ask her to contact us?" his mother cried into the phone.

"Mom, you have to understand, everything happened so fast, and normally I would be able to contact her every week or so. This mission was unlike anything else my team had ever undertaken and we didn't know until we were airborne that we wouldn't be able to contact anyone outside of ourselves. We didn't even have regular communication with our field CO, which is why it took them so long to rescue us. They didn't realize we were captured for several weeks, and by then we'd been moved out of the country temporarily."

"Son, are you okay?" his father asked in all seriousness.

"I will be, dad. Physically, I came out pretty good...much better than some of my other teammates. I lived." He heard his mother gasp and wished he could take the words back. He didn't want to worry her and he knew he'd just done that. "Mom, I'm fine. Now, for the reason I called...please say you'll forgive me for how this all went down and come to Montana next week? You'll adore Maddie. She's a wonderful girl from the South, a nurse at the cancer clinic up here in Castle Peaks, and I love her."

His father, the voice of reason, came back on the line, disconnecting the speakerphone, "Jeff, your mother and I wouldn't miss this opportunity to meet your wife for anything. We'll be there next Friday."

"Thanks, dad. Please know that I wanted to do things differently, circumstances just caught me by surprise. Is mom really upset?"

"She'll be fine once she has a chance to process everything you told us. I promise. Is there a hotel...?"

"Don't worry about where you're going to stay. I've made some friends in this small town and they're taking care of everything. Just get yourselves here."

"You've got it. See you soon, son."

His father disconnected the call and Jeff sat back on the couch, breathing a sigh of relief. *One down, one to go.*

Chapter 14

Jeff closed his eyes for a moment, praying for wisdom and guidance for the next call he was going to make. After several minutes, he opened his eyes and pushed up off the couch. Maddie kept a written phone directory in the drawer next to her bed and he knew her parents' phone numbers were listed in there. This was supposed to be a surprise, so he couldn't very well ask her for her mom and dad's phone number.

He'd already chanced blowing the surprise when he'd snuck her simple gold wedding band off the dresser the day before and driven over to Evansville to see the small jeweler there. He really wanted to upgrade her wedding ring, but after speaking with both Trent and Bryan and getting their advice, he'd abandoned the idea of completely replacing her ring, choosing instead to find a complimentary setting that could be joined with her original band.

He'd chosen a simple diamond setting that would sit atop the simple band and had a drape of small diamonds that wound curl around the lower band. The jeweler had already sized the new band, with a promise to solder the two bands together whenever they could get back over to Evansville for a few hours. Trent had discussed things with Sara, and unbeknownst to Maddie, she had two weeks of vacation time she would be taking right after the wedding.

Jeff planned to fly back to Georgia with her parents, spend a week there, and then fly to Salt Lake City and spend another week showing Maddie around his hometown, before returning to Castle Peaks. He hoped by the time they returned he would have a better idea of the direction he wanted to go with his future. Right now, he had intentionally pushed those decisions to the back of the pile.

Taking a deep breath, he sat down on the couch and punched in the numbers for Maddie's parent's home. He knew her dad was getting ready to retire and that her mother hadn't worked for the last several years. She'd been a nurse in the local school system and had retired after working more than thirty-years at her job. Maddie had gotten her love for medicine and her compassion from her parents and Jeff was looking forward to telling them what a good job they had done raising her. She was the woman she was today because of them and he still had trouble sometimes believing that she'd chosen to spend the rest of her life with him.

He pushed the last number and then waited, not realizing he was holding his breath until a gentle voice answered on the other end.

"Grantham residence."

Jeff sucked in a breath and felt his palms grow damp. *I can't believe how nervous I am. I don't get sweaty palms when I'm ambushing the enemy!*

"Hello? Is anyone there?"

Jeff cleared his throat, "Uhm…yes, ma'am. I'm here."

"Can I help you?" the woman asked.

Jeff thought how much she sounded like her daughter, or was it the other way around? "Ma'am, my name is Jeff Young and I was hoping I could speak with you for a few minutes. I know your daughter, Maddie."

"You're a friend of Maddie's? Is everything alright? We haven't heard from her much over the last year or so. Is she doing okay?"

"She's fine. I'm sorry she hasn't been in better communication with you, I'm afraid that's partly my fault."

"I don't understand," the woman told him with suspicion in her voice.

"Let me back up for a minute. Is your husband home, by chance?"

"No, he's already left for work. Jeff, what is this about?"

"Ma'am, I don't quite know how to say this. I thought it would be easier, but I was wrong."

"Son, I don't know you, but sometimes just putting whatever you have to say out there is the only avenue that makes sense."

"Okay. I get that. Mrs. Grantham, I love your daughter."

"Well, I must say that wasn't what I was expecting to hear. Maddie hasn't mentioned anything about a boyfriend…"

"Well, that's probably because I'm not her boyfriend, I'm her husband. Now, I realize this is a shock and all, and I promise there is a good explanation for why you and your husband weren't told this many months ago…I would really love a chance to meet you and explain everything. In person. But that isn't possible right now and I'm trying to make things right by your daughter."

"Jeff…I don't know quite what to say. This information is very disturbing to me and frankly, if my husband were here, you'd be getting an earful about now."

"I realize that, and again, I apologize. Let me try to explain. I met Maddie at the Army base in Colorado Springs while my team was there on a small Stateside assignment."

"Your team? Are you in the military, then?"

"Yes, ma'am. Special Forces. Anyway, I had to go to the hospital for some stitches, and that's where I met your daughter. To say she knocked me off my feet would be an understatement. I fell in love with her almost immediately. We dated for quite a few weeks before I asked her to marry me. We were planning to get married in the Fall, but Uncle Sam had different ideas. My team was suddenly called upon for a special mission and we were barely given a week's notice. The mission was only supposed to last two months, but I couldn't stand the thought of leaving Maddie without my ring on her finger.

"In my line of work, there is always the chance that something will go wrong and I wanted to make sure Maddie was taken care of to the best of my ability if that happened. We got married by the local judge and a few days later I shipped out. We talked about the fact that neither of our parents knew we were even dating anyone, and decided as soon as I returned we would take a few trips and tell you all in person."

"What changed that? I have to tell you I would have much preferred to hear this directly from my daughter's lips."

Jeff nodded his head, "I realize that, but something went terribly wrong on this mission. We were in deep cover behind enemy lines and our communication with the rest of the military was very minimal and infrequent. We didn't know any of this until we were already headed for the Middle East. Anyway, things went south and my entire team was captured. It took them well over five months to find us and rescue us."

Jeff paused, trying not to let his mind slip into memories of those months. He needed to keep his wits about him and finish this conversation. "We had no communication with the United States government and Maddie was left on the base, wondering each day when she was going to hear from me again. The base CO didn't even know what was happening with my team and upon his advice, she found something outside of the military to keep her mind busy. That's why she took the job in Castle Peaks, Montana."

"I wondered why she left a job she seemed to love in Colorado to go to a small town in Montana."

"That's why, but she absolutely loves it here. I came straight here upon returning to the States, and I quickly realized that we did our families a disservice by not trying to include you in our earlier wedding. Maddie says she's okay with things, but I know it weighs on her mind how to tell you and her dad about us."

"Yes, I can see how that would be hard for her. She's never liked disappointing people, especially her father and I."

"She thinks we are going to fly out there in a few weeks to surprise you, but I have other plans in the works. I've made a few friends here in Castle Peaks and they've been helping me put together the wedding she always dreamed of. She doesn't know a thing about it, but part of that plan includes having both sets of parents in attendance next Saturday."

"Next Saturday?! But that's only a week and a half away!"

"Ma'am, I know it's short notice, but I was really hoping you and your husband would use the airline tickets I've already purchased and fly out here. Everything is already arranged, and I want Maddie to have a wedding she'll always remember. Being away from one another for almost nine months right after we got married was hard on her, and I'm aiming to do everything I can to show her how much she means to me. "

"It sounds like you love her, son."

"I do. I never actually believed in love at first sight until I met her, but I truly believe God sent her to Colorado Springs just for me."

"You're a believer, then?" Maddie's mom asked.

"Yes, ma'am."

"Please call me Catherine and stop with the ma'am stuff. It makes me feel much older than I know I am."

"Catherine, thank you. My parents will be driving up from Utah next Friday. I've purchased tickets from Atlanta to Boise for you and your husband. Someone will meet you there and drive you to Castle Peaks."

"This is such a surprise…"

"I realize that and I'm only sorry I wasn't able to speak with you and your husband this morning. I had to wait until Maddie left for work to make this call."

"Maddie loves surprises," Catherine told him. "She always did. When most kids were trying to sneak into their Christmas presents, she was always proud of the fact that she wanted to be completely surprised come Christmas morning."

"That sounds like the Maddie I've come to love and know. I look forward to hearing more about her childhood. I've arranged for her to have the two weeks following our wedding off and I've already purchased tickets for us to fly back to Georgia with you and your husband. I look forward to seeing where she grew up and getting to you know you both."

"Well, you seem to be going to a lot of trouble to fix things."

"Catherine, it was never my intention to keep our relationship a secret, but after I was deployed I found out we were to have no contact with anyone until the mission was complete. I had no way to contact Maddie…they wouldn't even let us send letters to our families."

"Your parents were okay with this?" she asked.

"No, but I've been doing this job a while and they realize that no communication from me means I'm working. As long as uniformed men didn't show up, they knew I was still alive and would contact them as soon as I was able to. I'm not saying they liked this arrangement, but they were at least used to it. Maddie never had a chance to get used to me being gone for so long; leaving to come to Montana kept her sane during those long months."

"I can't believe she didn't say anything. Granted, we've only talked a few times in the last year, but I'm hurt she didn't say anything."

"She knew you and your husband would want to meet me and she wasn't in a position to make that happen, or even give you a timeframe for when that might be possible. She was afraid you would think badly of me."

Jeff waited for a response, drumming his fingertips on his thigh as silence prevailed for several long minutes. Finally, Catherine Grantham spoke again. "Jeff, do you love my daughter?"

"Yes, with all of my heart."

"And are you going to be leaving her again in the near future?"

"I was given three months' furlough by my CO. I have to make some decisions about the future before that time is up, and right now, I can't say that I have any answers. I know I love your daughter and the thought of leaving her again breaks my heart."

Catherine Grantham made a small noise and then spoke again, "We'll be there next week. I'll explain things to my husband, but be prepared to make your own explanations when we arrive. We just want the best for our daughter, and if marriage to you is what makes her happy, then we'll give you our support. One hundred percent."

Jeff felt relief flow over him and he offered up a silent prayer of thanksgiving. "I can't wait to meet you and your husband."

"Wesley. My husband's name is Wesley and I know he'll thank you to use it."

"I'll keep that in mind. I'm having the airline tickets delivered directly to your home." He then gave her his personal cell phone with instructions to contact him immediately if they didn't arrive the next day. There was only one more thing he had to ask, and he was hoping it wasn't going to be too much of an imposition. It was Maddie's dream, one she'd foregone to marry him and he wanted to make it come true if possible.

"Catherine, there is one more request I would like to make. Maddie told me about her childhood dream of the perfect wedding, and in it she always said how she wanted to get married in your wedding dress, but that wasn't a possibility any longer. Could I ask why that is?"

Catherine started laughing, "Well, that would be easy to explain. Jeff, I'm only 5'2" tall and as you're very aware, Maddie is significantly taller than I am. There are also several dress sizes difference between us. Wearing my dress became an impossibility around the time she entered the sixth grade and outgrew me."

Jeff sighed, "Oh."

"I know she probably dreamed of wearing my dress...does she have one picked out...or did she have one when you married the first time?"

"No, she just wore a simple dress she already had in her closet...things went so quickly. Some of the staff at the clinic are arranging things...Maddie thinks there is a fundraiser that includes a fashion show and she's been asked to play the bride in a photo shoot. We have a dress designer bringing a variety of gowns up Saturday morning for her to find one that fits perfectly, but I know the ladies are hoping to have something specifically planned out for her and mostly sized correctly before then."

"Why don't I send you a picture of my wedding dress and they could find something similar? I have the veil I wore...do you think Maddie would want to wear it?"

"That is the perfect idea! Catherine, I want your daughter to smile so much next Saturday that her face hurts at the end of the day.

Please, bring the veil with you and if you could just text me a picture of the dress, I'll make sure it gets to the right people."

"I can't tell you how happy it makes me to see you doing so much to make my daughter happy. I'll send you the picture right away and I'll go get the veil out of the attic as soon as we get off the phone. Thank you for caring so much for my daughter."

"Thank you for raising such an amazing woman. I look forward to saying that in person next week. Please let me know if those tickets don't arrive tomorrow."

"I will. Jeff…thank you for calling. I know this couldn't have been an easy phone call to make, but it shows you are a man of character and I couldn't be happier to know that my daughter married a man of integrity and conscience."

Jeff felt humbled by her praise and mumbled a goodbye. He disconnected the call and then sagged back against the couch. That had not been an easy call to make, but it was done and now he could relax and look forward to the future. He grinned as he put Maddie's phone directory back in the drawer. *She's not going to know how to respond next Saturday when she sees her dad standing at the back of the church, ready to escort her down the aisle. I need to speak with Trent about having someone film the ceremony. This is definitely something we're going to want to remember.*

Chapter 15

March 2nd, Thursday, Nine days before the wedding…

Maddie finished changing out nine-year old Tucker Dawson's IV and then smiled at him, "You did good, bud. Now, what would you like to do while we wait for those fluids to run in?" Tucker had been at the clinic for almost a month now, and so far he was responding very well to the treatments designed to rid his body of the cancer cells that had been found in his femur.

He'd been a happy little boy who loved soccer until he'd fallen during a game and ended up with a broken leg. The leg had required a surgical fix, and that was when the surgeon had noticed an abnormality in the bone tissue around the break. An orange-sized tumor had cause his femur to become unstable, causing the break. They had removed what malignant tissue they could, then stitched him back up and arranged for him to come to the Mercer-Brownell clinic for further treatment.

As the oldest child of five, and having only a mother at home to care for him and his siblings, his treatment had been very strenuous on everyone involved. Thanks to the generous donations that were made to the clinic each year, Tucker's treatment wasn't costing his mother a dime, but she needed to work and so she was only able to be at the clinic on the weekends. Each Friday evening, she would load the other four children up into her beat-up old station wagon and drive the six hours to Castle Peaks to spend the weekend with her son.

She would then leave Sunday evening, right after dinner, and drive back home to work a full week and do it all over again. The nurses and staff at the clinic had taken the younger children under their wings, as well as the young mother, who just recently celebrated her thirtieth birthday. If everything went as planned, Tucker would be allowed to go back home in a few days, and only need to return to the clinic once a month for the next year to monitor his progress.

His story was one of the happy ones, and his clever brain and spontaneous laughter would be missed, but in a good way. He was one of the lucky ones and any tears shed when he left would be tears of joy.

Maddie looked at her young charge once more and then suggested, "How about I go find a friend for you to play a game with? I think Emily was here earlier. Would you like me to see if she's still around and wants to play?"

Tucker immediately nodded his head and Maddie patted his shoulder, "I'll see what I can do to make that happen." She made a few notations in his chart and then left the room, heading for the breakroom to see if Emily was still around.

She didn't find Emily, but she did find Tori, Sara, Jess and Alaina all seated around a table, appearing to be making lists of some sort. "Hey, what are y'all up to?" Maddie heard the Southern twang come out of her voice and realized she'd forgotten to check her speech.

Sara and the others smiled indulgently at her and Sara commented, "Our little Southern belle...I love it when you talk like that. And, we're not doing anything. Are you still on shift?"

Maddie nodded, "For another two hours. I was actually looking for Emily. Tucker has at least another forty-five minutes on his IV bag and was wondering if she might want to play a board game with him?"

Tori smiled, "She's in the other building bugging the new interns, but I'm sure she'd love to play with Tucker. I'll call over there and have someone send her this direction."

Maddie smiled, "Thanks. Interns?" she asked Sara.

Sara nodded, "We're going to be starting an outreach clinic in California that specifically targets the homeless who've been diagnosed with some sort of cancer. They'll be referred to us by a variety of agencies, but finding qualified physicians to tend to them was becoming problematic. After discussing it, Dr. Jackson and Dr. Michael both agreed it would be beneficial to have those interested train up here for three to six months before heading back to California."

Maddie smiled, "Hands on experience will be good for them. How many of them are there?"

"Six right now. If everything seems to work fine, we'll take another six when they leave."

Jess smiled, "This program is going to save so many lives."

Maddie nodded at her former roommate, "It's a great concept and I agree with you. Well, duty calls. See y'all later."

Sara and the others waved to her and Maddie stepped out of the room, getting the sense that she'd just missed something. She wasn't sure what it was, but it had definitely seemed like she'd been the only one not in on the joke. She almost went back into the room to ask for an explanation, but right then, Emily came bouncing into the clinic with the Battleship game in her arms.

"Hey, Miss Maddie. I heard Tucker wanted to play?"

Maddie smiled at her, "He sure does. Go on into his room and I'll see if I can round up some cookies for the two of you."

Emily grinned, "Awesome!"

Maddie agreed, this place was pretty awesome and she felt privileged to work here. She went back to checking on the remainder of her patients, already looking forward to the evening Jeff had planned for them. There was a movie theater over in Evansville and

113

as soon as she got off work, they were going to drive over there and eat dinner and see a movie.

She was excited to spend some alone time with him and found herself watching the clock repeatedly, as the last two hours of her shift crawled by. 3 o'clock couldn't come soon enough for her.

*****

Sara waited until Maddie had left the room and then she breathed out a sigh of relief and a small giggle, "That was close!"

"Tell me about it," Jess told her in a laugh of her own. "I had the wedding dresses we picked out sitting right in front of me."

The four women shared a sigh of relief and then got back to business. "Okay, Maddie's parents have been apprised of the situation by Jeff and will be flying in next Friday evening. Bill Mercer offered to let them stay in one of his guest rooms, as well as Jeff's parents."

"That's really nice of Bill," Tori commented.

"He's a nice guy and his housekeeper is fantastic as well. Trent is going to find someone to pick Mr. and Mrs. Grantham up in Bozeman and drive them this direction. They won't get here until late, but that's okay. Less chance of Maddie finding out they're here.

"Jeff's parents are driving up and will be getting here in the early afternoon that day. I'm going to come up with some reason I need Maddie to help me with the girls to keep her out of town while his parents get settled."

The others nodded, "Well, I spoke to the florist and she's going to bring the flowers to the church Saturday morning around 10 o'clock. That will give us a few hours to get everything set just right." Tori had asked to be put in charge of the flowers and decorations inside the church. She had an eye for decorating and everyone else was pleased to hand her the task.

"What about the cake for the reception?" Sara asked, marking the flowers off of her to-do list.

"Jane and Samuel are flying in Wednesday morning. I already spoke with Tamara over at the diner and she said Jane was welcome to use anything in the kitchen. Jane's bringing any specialty ingredients with her."

"Are they flying commercial?" Sara asked.

Tori shook her head, "No, I believe they are flying in with Dr. Michael." At the mention of Sara's brother-in-law, all four women sobered and looked to her. "Any word on Grace?"

Sara shook her head, holding back tears of frustration on her sister's behalf. Since finding a lump under her arm nearly two weeks ago now, Grace had been preparing herself for the worst. "Jackson has been having daily lab work drawn, but her white cell count seems to be within normal limits."

Tori smiled, "That's good, right?"

Sara nodded, "Yes, but it still doesn't answer the question as to whether or not the lump is something to be concerned about. Michael wants to biopsy it, just to be on the safe side, but Grace's blood pressure has been high and he's afraid to give her any anesthesia. She has almost no pain tolerance and could never stand for the biopsy to occur without something to numb the area."

Tori shivered, "Believe me, she doesn't want to try it without." Tori had survived breast cancer and knew all too well how painful some procedures could be. "Is the baby doing okay?"

Sara nodded, "Yes, for now. Jackson ordered a special ultrasound wand that will let him, or Michael, physically see the baby, even now. It will be here the day after tomorrow and I imagine using it will be one of the first things Michael will do when he gets here."

"Well, hopefully she can try to relax and just be happy the baby is doing so well."

"She'll feel better once she knows what's up with the lump. It's not changed in size, not that she can tell. Honestly, I don't know what to think right now."

"We'll just keep praying for a good report and outcome," Tori told her.

Sara nodded and then looked back down at her list, "Okay, the only thing left on this list is the accommodations for Jeff's teammates. Anyone got any ideas? There are at least five of them."

Everyone was quiet for a few moments and then Jess suggested, "How about the Showalter's house? It's sitting empty and has six bedrooms."

Sara considered it for a minute and then asked, "Do you know how to get ahold of them?"

Jess nodded, "I have their contact information in my phone. Shall I give them a call?"

Sara nodded and Jess did so, waiting patiently for Mr. Showalter to answer.

"Hello?"

"Mr. Showalter, this is Jessame in Castle Peaks."

"Jess! How are you, hon?"

"I'm good, Mr. Showalter. Real good. How is Mrs. Showalter?"

"We're both doing fine, dear. The weather down here is beautiful, as always."

Jess grinned and then stated the reason for her call, "Mr. Showalter I was calling for a reason. Do you remember meeting a nurse named Maddie when you were home last? She works in the children's clinic."

WAITING FOR LOVE'S RETURN

"Why yes. A lovely little red-headed girl."

"That's her. Well, she's married to a military man who has been deployed for almost a year and he's now home. They rushed to get married when he got his deployment orders and never had a proper wedding. We're all...the entire town practically...is pulling together to help her husband surprise her with the wedding of her dreams this coming Saturday."

"Well, now! That sounds mighty nice. Saturday, you said. That's only a week away."

"Yes and that's why I'm calling. Jeff Young, her husband, has invited his fellow military teammates to attend, but there are five of them and no one else has any spare rooms left. I was wondering if you would allow us to use your vacant home for a few nights. I would personally see that everything was taken care of and such."

"Military men, you said?"

"Yes sir, Special Forces. Jeff was their team leader on their last mission, where they were captured and held for many months before being rescued."

"Those boys are mighty brave and the missus and I would be honored to have them use the house. I'll call the housekeeper we use when in residence today and have her go open up the house and stick around to act as a cook for them."

"Really? Mr. Showalter, that's an amazing offer." Jess looked up and could see Sara smiling and writing stuff down quickly. "Do you need me to do anything from this end?"

"Just tell those boys thank you for me and my wife. We sure do appreciate all that they do for this country."

Jess nodded her head, "I'll be sure to tell them that. Thank you again."

"No thanks necessary. How's that new husband of yours?"

"Doing well, sir. I'm very happy."

"I look forward to meeting him when I get there in May."

"I look forward to it as well, sir. Thank you again."

"You're very welcome. See you in a few months."

Jess hung up the phone and made a victory sign over her head with her arms, "Score one for our team. All accommodations are now accounted for."

Sara grinned, "That means the only thing left to do is the dresses. I have a designer who said he could bring up a bunch of dresses if we could get him her approximate size…"

"How are you going to get Maddie to try on a wedding dress?" Tori asked, still wondering how they were going to pull this part of the wedding off.

Alaina had been fairly quiet up to this point, but now she spoke up, "I hope I didn't overstep my bounds, but Jeff stopped me yesterday when I was helping out at the church and he came up with a really good idea."

Sara waved her on, "Let's hear it. It can't be worse than the ones I've come up with."

Alaina looked around the room and then whispered, "He thinks we should tell her we're doing a fashion show to help raise money for the clinic. That would explain the decorating and the need for a hairstylist and makeup person…We could tell her a photographer was going to come take pictures of nurses and caretakers dressed up in various types of clothing and that with her vibrant hair, she had been selected to play the bride and wear the wedding dress for the photo shoot. We could tell her they have a variety of dresses to choose from, but Jeff has a picture of the one her mom wore and asked me if we could try to pick something out similar to it."

"But if she's going to get to choose..."

"We just make sure the only dress that will really fit is the one that looks closest to the one her mom wore. I think it could work. Jeff said her mom is bringing her own veil for Maddie to wear."

The room was silent and then the women shared a look and all started smiling, "Alaina, that is a brilliant idea. Simply brilliant."

Alaina grinned, "Actually, all of the credit goes to Jeff for this one. I think it's really sweet that he's doing this for her."

Sara looked at her as she picked up on the wistfulness in her voice, but she didn't question the newest member of their staff. Alaina was only twenty-three and had only been with them a few short weeks. In that time, she'd proven to be a competent nurse, and while she never withheld her care from the adult patients, she balked at working in the children's side of the clinic. There was something almost tragic in her eyes at those times, and Sara made a mental note to dig a little deeper into the young woman's past as soon as the wedding was over with.

Castle Peaks had healed many a broken person, both in body and in spirit. If one of the members of the Mercer-Brownell clinic was hurting, she couldn't just ignore their pain and allow them to suffer. Whatever had happened in the young woman's past could be dealt with and hopefully she could find peace or at least forgiveness. Sara was certainly going to try.

They adjourned the meeting a few minutes later, a plan in place to snare themselves a bride for the wedding of the year about to take place in a week. Maddie would play the bride beautifully, and her maids' of honor and attendants could be dressed in matching colors of dresses, whether or not they matched in style or material. Things were coming together and Sara couldn't wait to see Maddie's face when she was driven to the church and escorted inside.

She's going to cry. I'm going to cry. Shoot, I bet the entire town will be crying by the time she gets down the aisle. So be it. Weddings and funerals deserve tears, albeit for different reasons. She had no intention of attending a funeral anytime soon, so a wedding it would be. The entire town had grieved over Annsley's death, but this would be time to celebrate. Something they all needed right now. Especially her sister.

Chapter 16

March 6th, Monday morning, the week of the wedding...

Jeff was working hard on getting the ground ready for the solarium. The church had already had the perfect covered courtyard, and with the structural aspects of the space handled, the project had moved forward at lightning speed. Finding the proper plants and materials in the middle of the winter had been a difficult task, but he'd finally found a few greenhouses in the deep South that were willing to ship things up to them, without waiting for the weather to warm up.

A large shipment of plants was due to arrive the following day, and he and a crew of six other church parishioners, were busily trying to get the ground ready for planting. They'd already cleared the area, brought in a rototiller and ripped the hard dirt up to make it easier to incorporate the peat moss and compost material, and luckily, they'd found a rancher over in Evansville who had a large compost pile he didn't mind selling part of.

Out of respect for the church members, they'd waited until early this morning to bring those materials in and he only hoped the smell would dissipate before any kind of church services were held in the chapel again. Currently, the smell of a barnyard permeated the entire church building along with the smell of freshly dug dirt.

"It's supposed to be in the high 50's today, maybe we should go through the church and open up all of the windows and door and aerate the place out," Jeb from the drugstore suggested.

Jeff nodded, "That's not a bad idea. When Pastor Jameson gets back I'll run that idea by him, but it sounds good to me."

"How many rose bushes are coming in?" Cora, Bill Mercer's housekeeper, called from the far side of the solarium.

"A dozen in varying colors. Why?" Jeff asked, making his way across the soft dirt to where she and several other women stood waiting for his answer.

"Well, rose bushes need some special attention if we want them to do well and bloom properly. We're going to add some bone meal to each of the planting sites to get them going."

"Ladies, Pastor Jameson is lucky to have your knowledge. If there's anything else that needs to be done to make sure these plants thrive, just let me know. If we don't have it, I'll find it for you. I have some friends driving over from Colorado Springs tomorrow and there are several large greenhouses and supply stores in Denver. It would be no problem at all for them to pick up anything we might have forgotten."

Cora beamed at him, "Jeff, I surely do look forward to meeting your parents. They raised a good man."

Jeff blushed a bit and nodded, "Thanks. I'm not sure my mother has quite forgiven me for not telling her sooner that I'd gotten married..."

"Pshaw! You did what you thought was right at the time, and a little lesson I learned a long time ago," Cora told him with a smile, "Don't apologize for following your own path. People have expectations, and often think things should have happened in a certain order or at a certain time, but we aren't responsible for their disappointments. As long as we are following the path we believe is correct and do our best to live our lives in a way that is pleasing to the Lord, we don't owe anyone any apology."

Jeff grinned at the older woman, "That's a mighty strong stance, Miss Cora."

"Well, it's true. I spent my younger years doing what I thought everybody else expected me to do and I was miserable. Now, I live my life for me and as long as God's okay with the choices I make, everyone else can either be okay with it or keep it to themselves."

Jeff barked out a laugh, "That is a great life philosophy. I may just have to borrow that."

"Don't borrow it, take it as your own. You and Maddie will be much happier in the long run for it."

Pastor Jameson arrived at that moment and saw Cora talking to him. He called out as he crossed the open space, "Miss Cora, you aren't filling this young man's head with your years of wisdom are you?"

"You know I am."

Jeff greeted the Pastor, "Good morning, Pastor. Sorry about the place smelling like a barnyard."

Pastor Jameson laughed, "Well, if it still smells like this come Sunday, I'll just have to work it into my sermon."

Everyone laughed and nodded, "That might get some people's attention, Pastor."

"We'll see. I just came from the hospital and I thought you might all want to keep Grace in your prayers. As most of you know, there is some concern that she might have found what could be cancer, but the doctors have been unable to fully check things out because of the danger to her unborn child. This has caused a significant amount of stress on her and as of this morning, she's been admitted to the clinic for around the clock supervision. Her blood pressure has spiked and there seems to be some abnormality with the heartbeat of the baby.

"Her husband has been notified and he is flying up here this morning. She's refused to let anyone examine her until he gets here."

Jeff nodded and reached for his phone, "Excuse me, will you?" He knew Maddie was at the hospital and he hoped that maybe she could be a levelling force for the scared woman. Maddie and Grace seemed to get along very well together, and he knew that Grace had told Maddie about her pregnancy, and finding the lump, before she'd even spoken to her husband about either.

"Maddie? Hey, have you got a minute?"

"Hi. Yes, I have a few minutes. You sound different."

"I just spoke with Pastor Jameson…are you aware they admitted Grace this morning for observation?"

"No, I wasn't. I've been helping with chemo treatments in the children's clinic all morning. Is everything alright?"

"I guess not. Something about an irregular heartbeat and her blood pressure being elevated. Anyway, she's refusing to let anyone examine her further until her husband gets here, but he's flying in from California. It could be a while."

Maddie sighed, "I'll get over there and see her as soon as I can get away from here. Dr. Mike will probably arrive on the private jet his family owns so he should be here in a few short hours. I assume Sara is over there with her now, but I'll check things out. Thanks for calling me."

"No problem. You and she seemed to be friends and I thought you would want to know."

"We are and I do. Thanks again. How are things going over at the church?"

"Well, besides the smell, things seem to be going well."

Maddie chuckled, "I warned you what bringing in fresh compost was going to smell like. I grew up living next to a dairy farm. When the wind would shift, the entire neighborhood would smell like a stable."

"Yeah, but it had to be done. Plants are arriving tomorrow, speaking of which...I know you told me, but I seem to have forgotten. What's your schedule for the rest of the week?"

"I'm working every day and I agreed to pull a double shift on Thursday so that Alaina could go into Boise. I'm not sure why, but it seemed fairly important and everyone else already had plans for their day off."

"That's rather nice of you," Jeff commented, smiling as another piece of their surprise came together. Maddie's parents' flight had been changed and in order to get them here in time for them to be well rested for the wedding, he'd had to change their flight to Thursday instead of Friday. Alaina had generously offered to pick them up since she was planning to be in Boise anyway. Everything was working out just fine and Jeff was only hoping it would continue to do so throughout the remainder of the week.

"I'm a nice person. See you at dinner?"

"Yeah. I'll even try to get home before you and wash some of this cow smell off of me."

"I would appreciate that. I'll go check on Grace."

"Okay. Catch you later. Love you."

"Love you, too."

Jeff pocketed his phone and turned to see that he'd become the center of attention for those working on the solarium. "What?"

They all just smiled and shook their heads, turning back to their respective tasks with more energy than before. The grand opening of the solarium was planned for Saturday, when it would be dedicated to the memory of Annsley and used to host the wedding reception at the same time. Annsley's parents were coming up for the wedding ceremony and to be there for the dedication, and it was just another confirmation that Jeff was doing the right thing.

He couldn't wait for Saturday to arrive, but in the meantime, there was much work to be done. "Alright, what's next?"

Chapter 17

Later that morning…

Maddie finished notating her last patient's chart and then marked herself out on break. Sara wandered through the department and Maddie stopped her to ask about Grace

"She's just being stubborn," Sara told her.

"She's scared. Is her blood pressure dangerously high?"

Sara shook her head. "No, but she almost fainted this morning at breakfast. She wouldn't even let them draw blood!"

"But her husband is coming and she's here. If something else happens, there are people here to deal with it."

"I guess. I know she's scared, but something has to be done or she's going to worry herself sick and possibly harm the baby."

"Have you told her that?" Maddie asked kindly.

"She knows. She's done this before and she's been around enough nurses to know you don't take chances with certain things. I don't know how we're going to do this for another five weeks. That's how long the obstetrician Mike brought with him thinks she needs to wait before undergoing anesthesia."

"Five weeks? That's not really all that long."

"To her it is."

Maddie nodded. "I can see that. And there's no way they can biopsy before then?"

"Not without anesthesia. They could do a local numbing, but it looks like they would have to go in almost an inch to reach the lump, and a local won't numb that deep. Grace doesn't handle pain well at all."

"How did she deliver Daniella?"

"She had a C-section and they gave her an epidural. She didn't feel a thing."

"Okay, there has to be something they could use. What about hypnosis?"

"What about it?"

"Well, when I was doing my clinical rotations, there was a study going on at the hospital where I worked. It was about using hypnosis to put people into a trance-like state where they didn't need anesthesia for certain benign procedures. Maybe this would fall into that category?"

"Hypnosis…That's a really interesting idea. I'm going to mention it to Mike when he gets here. I'm assuming he hasn't heard anything about it or he would have already suggested it. What hospital was the research being done at? I'd like to print off some of the research for him before he arrives, so he can make an informed decision before he suggests it. If he suggests it."

"I was interning at Emory Hospital, but they were working in conjunction with John Hopkins out of Maryland."

"That makes sense," Sara told her with a smile. "I'll see what I can find out. Thanks for mentioning this."

"Do you think Grace would mind if I stopped by to see her?"

"I think she'd love it, especially if you just stopped by to talk and not to try and convince her to let us poke her with needles and the like."

"I'll discreetly monitor her and I won't mention any medical procedures."

"Thanks, Maddie."

"You're welcome." Maddie headed over to the other building, greeting fellow staff members as she went. She always tried to keep a positive spirit and a smile upon her face, and today she was hoping she could bring a smile to Grace's face as well.

She rapped her knuckles on the door, then entered the room to see Grace sitting on the side of the hospital bed, a frown on her face and unshed tears in her eyes. "Hey, Grace. I heard you were paying us a small visit."

"Maddie, if you came in here to convince me to—"

"Whoa! I just came by to see if you wanted to head down to the cafeteria with me for a snack. It's not quite lunchtime yet, but I've been here since 7:30 this morning and I need something to tide me over until my lunch break."

Grace gave her a suspicious look. "You're not here to try and draw my blood?"

"Well, I could if that's what you like, but I'd rather go see if they have chocolate yogurt in the frozen yogurt machine today."

Grace shook her head. "I'm sorry. It's just that everyone wants to poke and prod at me and I just want to wait until Mike gets here."

"No, I get it. You trust him and don't want to find out anything unless he's by your side. There's nothing wrong with that. I heard he should be arriving shortly."

Grace nodded, "He landed in Boise half an hour ago and is already on the highway."

"Well, then. How about that frozen yogurt?"

Grace smiled and the tension in her shoulders seemed to disappear momentarily. "That sounds really good. Now, are you going to fight me on walking on my own two feet?"

Maddie appeared to consider the question for a moment, then asked, "Sara said you almost fainted this morning and you and I both know how dangerous fainting in the hallway would be for your baby. I tell you what. Why don't you let me take your blood pressure and if it's in the normal range, you can walk right beside me. If it's high, you let me show off my mad wheelchair driving skills."

Grace laughed at the funny face she made and nodded her head. "That sounds like a deal I can take. I really do feel better now."

"I'm glad." Maddie made short work of taking her blood pressure, and unfortunately it was high. Not dangerously so, but higher than she would have liked for a woman in her first trimester of pregnancy.

Sara and Mike found them in the cafeteria forty-five minutes later, laughing at a story Grace was telling about Daniella and her first experience in the snow. She'd only been four when she'd first come to Montana, and having been born and raised in Southern California, she'd never seen the white stuff. Maddie had met the little girl numerous times when she and her mom were visiting. She always followed her best friend Emily around the hospital. Emily seemed to walk on water where Daniella was concerned and Maddie often found herself eavesdropping on their conversation. They were usually very comical and full of five-year-old logic.

"Grace," Michael called her name as he leaned over her shoulder and kissed her on the cheek, "Sara tells me you almost fainted this morning?"

Grace turned around and allowed her husband to raise her to a standing position so that she could hug him properly. "I'm sure it was nothing, but they want to run some tests. I'm sorry you had to fly out here..."

"Don't be. I was coming out tomorrow anyway and just had to check on a few patients this morning. That's done and I'm here for the rest of the week."

Maddie watched their exchange, but then realized she'd been gone much longer than a normal break would last. "Grace, now that your husband has arrived, I really do need to get back to work."

"Thanks for coming to see me. It really did help to have something else to think about."

"No problem." She pushed away from the table and whispered to Sara, "Will you keep me updated on her condition?"

Sara nodded. "I found that information we discussed as well. I had Dr. Jackson look at it and he said it has real potential as an option for her. I even managed to get a phone number for one of the hypnotists that participated in the study. He lives in Denver now and is waiting on Mike to call him."

Maddie smiled. "That's good news. Let me know how things turn out."

Sara smiled. "I will. Thanks for easing her mind for a few minutes. If anyone gives you any trouble for being gone longer than normal, have them call me."

"I'm sure everything will be fine, but if not, I know who to call." Maddie headed back to the children's side of the clinic and finished her shift. Her mind remained on Grace, but when her shift ended and she walked over to check on her, she discovered that her husband had drawn her blood and ordered a few tests before taking her back to Trent and Sara's home.

Maddie saw that as a good sign and headed home herself. Things between her and Jeff were improving daily, and they were even starting to feel like a married couple now. They still hadn't discussed the hard stuff, but her nightmares hadn't returned and Jeff seemed to be more relaxed as each day passed. She was dreading the time when he would have to return to Colorado Springs just as much as she dreaded having to decide what she was going to do. She loved it here in Castle Peaks and really didn't want to leave, but Jeff couldn't do his job or lead his team from Montana.

She was still thinking about these heavy things when she arrived at the apartment and saw that Jeff was already home and in the shower. She methodically went through the motions of making dinner, starting a load of laundry, and sorting through the mail.

These were all normal activities, but the thoughts running around her head were anything but. Jeff immediately picked up on her lack of focus and, partway through dinner, he leveled her with a stare and asked her what was wrong.

"Nothing. Just a lot on my mind."

"About?" Jeff asked, putting his fork down and giving her his undivided attention.

Maddie did the same thing, trying to decide if she really wanted to get into this tonight. Jeff seemed willing to listen, but the last thing she wanted to do was upset the easy camaraderie they had developed over the last week or so.

"Maddie, talk to me. I can see that something is bothering you. Just tell me what it is."

Maddie sighed. "I guess I'm wondering what happens when your three months are up." She met his gaze and then looked away. She so badly wanted him to say he was staying wherever she was, but she also knew it wasn't fair to expect him to give up a career he'd had before they got married just because she was scared of him being gone or getting killed on the next mission.

Jeff was quiet for a minute and then suggested, "We probably should talk about the future. Why don't we finish dinner and I'll help you clean up and then we can talk as much as you want to?"

Maddie nodded. "Okay, that sounds good." They ate the rest of their meal in silence and washed and dried the dishes as a team, but no more talking was done other than the cursory words needed to complete their task. By the time they adjourned to the couch, Maddie was a ball of nerves, wishing she'd never brought the subject up.

Chapter 18

Jeff started the conversation. "So, what happens when my three months' furlough is up?" He'd insisted she sit beside him on the couch, and currently he was holding her hand, smoothing his thumb back and forth across the back of her knuckles in a way that she found comforting.

"You'll have to go back to Colorado Springs," she stated, trying to keep any emotion out of her voice.

Jeff nodded. "That's true. No matter what I decide, I will have to physically go back to Colorado Springs."

"Decide?' Maddie asked, keying in on the word that gave her a brief spark of hope.

"My current commitment to Uncle Sam will be up in three months' time. I think that's why Colonel Lents set that time limit. He knows I need to make some decisions and was making sure I had plenty of time to make them."

"I'm sorry, but I don't understand. There are time limits on your job?"

"Things changed in the military years ago, and now we actually sign up to stay in for certain periods of time. It used to be once you made an elite team, you were in until you asked to get out or were forced out." *Or until you died.* He didn't add that last part, not wanting to go there in this conversation. Not yet.

"So, if you signed up again, how long would you have to commit?" Maddie asked him. She could maybe handle a set time period. Maybe.

"Two or three years."

Jeff watched her for her reaction and didn't miss the way she flinched as she thought about having to risk losing him for another two or three years. She was scared and rightly so. The world he and his team worked in wasn't nice and didn't play by any rulebooks he'd ever seen. Things happened fast and the consequences were usually tough to swallow. It really wasn't any kind of life for someone so sweet and compassionate like Maddie to live, and he kind of hated the fact that he'd dragged her into his world.

"That's not forever…"

"But it is a long time. Frankly, I don't know that I can do it." She started to say something and he placed a finger over her lips. "Let me talk for a few minutes." When she nodded, he removed his finger and lifted her hand to his lips, kissing her fingers before returning it to his lap.

"This last mission…it was pure hell. My team and I had gotten good at getting into places where we weren't wanted and gathering intel. This time, we were supposed to also grab a key player in one of the jihadist groups operating in the region. We knew it was going to take a while to figure out how to get in and grab him, but until we were airborne, we didn't realize they were going to drop us in the middle of nowhere and we would have little to no contact with the outside world until the mission was over."

"Isn't that really dangerous?" Maddie asked, frowning.

"Yeah, and totally outside of protocol. That was when we also found out this operation wasn't exactly being sanctioned. We were on our own without a safety net."

"Shouldn't you have been given a choice?" she asked, horrified that he'd been put in such a position.

"We were, but when we saw what this guy was responsible for, none of us could walk away with a good conscience. Anyway, we had trouble from the get go. Equipment didn't work right and our sources on the ground were unreliable. Things went from bad to worse and we ended up walking right into a trap. They took all ten of us captive.

"It was bad, Maddie. They immediately transported us out of the country and moved us every ten days to two weeks. It was several weeks before anyone on this side knew there was a problem and by then, they were weeks behind in following our trail."

"They...what happened while you were held captive?" Maddie asked, squeezing his hand.

"It was bad and I'm not going to go into detail. I can't," he told her, looking at her with a plea in his eyes for her to take what he was willing to give her and let it go at that.

Maddie saw his plea and squeezed his hand again. "You don't have to tell me any of it, if you don't want to."

Jeff leaned over and kissed her tenderly. "Thank you for that. I need to tell you some of it...The men who held us figured out I was the highest ranking member of our team. They wanted information, but after working me over for a few days, they realized they weren't going to get anything from me. That's when they started working on the other members of the team. In front of me. It was horrible, and the hardest thing I've ever had to deal with.

"They tortured men I'd served with and called my friends...that were like a second family to me...but I couldn't tell them what they wanted to know. Not without betraying my country."

"I'm sure your teammates understood that."

Jeff nodded, "They begged me not to tell them anything...even as they were dying. I watched them torture and kill four of the best men I've ever served with..."

"And now you feel guilty because you lived and they didn't?" she asked.

WAITING FOR LOVE'S RETURN

"I did. I guess I still feel a portion of guilt, but I talked to several shrinks in Germany before they transported us home. The other guys who survived with me...they were there and they know I had no choice but to keep quiet. There were so many days I prayed they would just come get me and kill me...but then I would think about you and I would fight against that...I wanted to come home to you so badly."

Maddie was openly crying now. "I felt so alone the longer it went without getting any kind of word from you. I would see the women in the post office and at the commissary, and I could see the pity in their eyes. They all felt sorry for me and that made me feel sorry for myself. I hated feeling that way and decided to do something about it.

"When Colonel Lents suggested I find something to do away from the base, I know he was thinking about me joining a health club or taking up a craft of some sort...but I would have still been working on the base and seeing those women every day. When I saw the employment ad for the clinic, it seemed like a sign from above. Sara hired me over the phone."

"I'm so glad you found a way to cope with my absence. If I'd have known things were going to go as they did, I would have done things differently before I left." He watched Maddie's face fall and immediately knew she'd taken his words the wrong way.

"Hey, don't look like that. I would have still hustled you to the courthouse, but I would have made sure my parents knew you existed and asked them watch over you. I would have made sure your parents knew I loved their daughter and that she was going to need their support. I should have made sure you were taken care of."

Maddie shook her head, drying her tears. "We discussed this and wanted to tell our parents in person. Things just didn't work out as quickly as we would have liked. We can still tell them in person."

"And we will. I was thinking we could take a couple of trips over the next two months and maybe that would help me decide what I want to do. Colonel Lents offered me a trainer position at the base, but that would mean moving back to Colorado Springs. I can tell how much you really love it here."

"I do," Maddie told him with a smile. "It's kind of like a second home and I would hate to leave here, but my place is with you. You've made a career out of the military and I won't ask you to give it up."

Jeff was amazed by this woman he'd married. She was always so giving, even when her own happiness might be at stake. He loved knowing that she would give up her job here for him, but he was really hoping he could find a solution that would let her stay here and still allow him to make a living and support them both. So far, that hadn't presented itself, but then again, he hadn't really begun to look yet. *After we get back from visiting the parents, I'll get right on that. I'll have five weeks or so to find another career. Something will turn up if we're supposed to stay here.*

"So, while we're talking like this," Maddie began softly. "I started having nightmares a couple months after you left. About the time I moved up here."

"Nightmares? About what?" Jeff asked, liking the fact that she was opening up to him as well.

"About you. In each one of them you were hurt. They were horrible and I would wake up crying and scared...I finally talked to Pastor Jameson about them."

"And what did he say?" Jeff was kind of shocked to hear that she'd been having dreams about him hurting. That had been his life for most of his captivity, whether physically or emotionally.

"He said that maybe my dreams were a message and that the best thing I could do when I had them was to pray for you. For your safety and that of the men with you. I did that and the dreams didn't go away, but I felt better after I prayed."

Jeff pulled her into his arms, hugging her close. "Thank you for that. I needed those prayers over there so desperately. There were a few times when I didn't think I was going to live to see your face again. I missed you so much."

Maddie hugged him close, rubbing her cheek on his shirt. "Knowing what you went through...even just a little bit of it...I don't know that I can be as strong if you get sent overseas again."

Jeff rested his cheek against her head. "I don't know if I can risk being put into that position again. Several of my team members have already started the paperwork to discontinue their work for Uncle Sam. Without those guys to back me up...I don't know if I could go back into the field. We were like a family and it still hurts to know that some of them are never coming home."

Maddie held him tight. Even when he thought about putting some distance between them, she held onto him. "You don't have to make any decisions right now."

Jeff tipped her chin up and searched her eyes. "*We* don't have to make any decisions right now. We're in this together. I won't make any decisions you're not completely onboard with. This affects both of our lives and I don't want you to ever regret or resent me. Pastor Jameson thinks we should pray about things and I think he's right."

Maddie nodded. "I've learned that prayer seems to be the answer to lots of things. My mom is what I consider to be a prayer warrior. When anyone in the church needs something, she's the first one they call to intercede on their behalf. I grew up seeing her reading her Bible at the kitchen table and praying for this person or that situation. Sometimes, she'd sit there for hours, talking to God."

"You had a great example. My parents were both prayer warriors when I was growing up. I haven't exactly followed in their example, but over there…I did a lot of praying and I always felt more at peace with what was happening once I'd prayed. Almost like I wasn't alone anymore."

Maddie smiled at him. "You weren't. He promised never to leave us or forsake us. I think prayer helps remind us of that fact."

Jeff nodded and then tucked her cheek back against his chest. They stayed like that on the couch, quietly talking about anything and everything into the wee hours of the morning. They'd finally opened up to one another and suddenly it was as if the last nine months hadn't even happened. Gone was the nervous energy that had permeated the apartment from time to time, and in its place was a loving atmosphere with two people who wanted nothing more than to make the other happy. The love that had first brought them together was no longer just a smoldering ember, but a brightly burning fire.

Circumstances had tried to tear them apart, bringing doubt and second-guessing to their relationship, but love had won. Jeff held Maddie long after she had drifted off to sleep, his dreams filled with images of the future. It had already begun, and Saturday he would make sure the past was completely replaced with the wedding of her dreams. The wedding of his dreams, where he ended up with the most beautiful bride and a love that was blessed by Heaven above.

Chapter 19

March 7th, Tuesday afternoon...

It was becoming apparent to everyone that keeping the wedding a secret from Maddie would be much harder than they'd originally thought. Already she'd stopped by the diner on her way home from work and seen Jane and Samuel sitting in a booth. She'd never met either of them, but the fact that they were not regular townsfolk had her asking Tamara who they were.

"Oh, that's Trent's cousin, Jane. She used to live here but then she moved to San Diego and married Samuel. They come out here every so often to visit."

"Huh, I spoke to Sara several times today and she never mentioned having company."

Tamara nervously made up a story about their arrival, "Well, I guess they found out Dr. Mike was coming out here and decided to hitch a ride with him. They actually arrived yesterday."

"Oh, well, I'm sure with everything else going on, she didn't think about mentioning it. This fundraiser has everyone scrambling."

"How's that?" Tamara asked, trying to ignore the pointed looks and hand signals several of the other patrons were giving her behind Maddie's back.

"The fundraiser for the clinic on Saturday. I've been so busy I haven't really found out much about it, but all of the nursing staff was told we had to participate and that we were to present ourselves at the clinic promptly at 9 o'clock Saturday morning."

"I think it's good that the staff gets involved. I guess we won't be very busy around here on Saturday then. Maybe I'll come up there and see what's going on myself."

"You should. You work too much."

Tamara shook her head and huffed out a little laugh. "You're one to talk. Here's the pie you requested and I tucked in a few extra donuts for that hubby of yours. I hear he's been working hard over at the church."

"He's been there every day this week. Speaking of husbands, I need to get home and think about getting dinner ready."

"You do that, hon. See you later."

"Thanks for the donuts." Maddie waved goodbye to several other people who were either looking at menus or eating before she rushed home, anxious to get home and see her husband. Since the night before when they'd had their talk, she couldn't stop thinking about him. It was just as if they'd fallen in love all over again, and she had been planning a special dinner all day. She just needed to get home and get it cooked.

*****

Jeff and the crew were just finishing putting the last plants in the ground when he heard and sensed the arrival of his teammates. He turned, dusting his dirt-stained hands on his jeans and walked towards the five men who were more like brothers to him.

"Didn't know you had a green thumb, JC," his second in command and best friend, Derek Evans, called out. They greeted each other with a handshake that quickly turned into a hug and slapping of one another's backs.

Jeff greeted the rest of his team in a similar fashion, being careful of their healing injuries where needed. "Didn't you boys take gardening class after sniper school?"

"No, I guess we missed that. I surely didn't expect a church to smell like the back of a manure pile," Ian Tompkins stated.

Jeff laughed, "Well, coming from a cattle ranch, I'd guess you're an expert on that smell."

"You've got that right. I'm headed home next week. Already got my discharge paperwork signed. A week from now I'll be ankle deep in the stuff."

Jeff nodded his head. "I heard you were getting out. I heard that several of you were getting out." He looked at Derek. "You're the only one I haven't heard about yet."

Derek gave him a shrug. "I haven't decided yet. I'll let you know what I'm going to do about the same time you make up your mind."

Jeff shook his head. "I should have expected that from you."

Derek nodded. "I'm not staying in if you're out. I couldn't do it."

Jeff slapped his friend on the back. "We'll talk about this some more, but not here. Right now, since the muscle has arrived, how about you all help me set up those stone benches and fountains stacked outside the church?"

"The ones sitting in the snow?" Ezra Gayle asked, adjusting his crutches for a more stable support.

"Yeah, but you're not doing any of the lifting. In fact, why don't you get off your feet and you can supervise. I know you can read a map. Let's see how you do with a hastily drawn sketch." Jeff handed him the rough blueprints of where everything in the solarium was supposed to be placed and then led the other four men outside for the arduous task of moving the stone seating arrangements in.

He waited until they were out of earshot, then asked Derek, "How's his leg?"

"They had to pin it and his knee is never going to work right again. His discharge paperwork came through this morning before we left. He's heading back home to Hawaii right after the ceremony."

Jeff shook his head. "I'm glad he's getting out, I only hope he follows through on the physical therapy and gains some use of his knee back."

"They have a fairly decent VA hospital where he's headed. I figure I'll give him a few weeks and then check up on him."

"Thanks for doing that," Jeff told his best friend. These men were like brothers to him and Ezra's injuries had been the most significant. He'd been shot trying to get away at one point, and his torturers had cleaned the wound out, only to continually slice it open again and again. He'd developed a bone infection a few weeks before they'd been rescued, and the doctors at Ramstein Air Base in Germany had been forced to cut a significant portion of bone away to save his leg. The injury had been just above his knee, but the entire joint had been replaced, using a small piece of cadaver bone to help make up for the shortened femur that had been the result of the infection. Due to the pins holding everything together, he currently had no movement in that joint, and only time would tell if and when that might change.

"They're all doing better than could be expected. Owen and Austin are going to head back to the Northeast and fish on Owen's brother's boat. Neither one of them is ready for polite society, but a fishing boat will get them away from combat and give them a chance to come to terms with everything that happened over there. Therapy isn't doing the trick."

Jeff nodded his head, making a mental note to let each man know how much he appreciated serving with them over the last several years. His entire team was going in different directions, and he couldn't blame them. He, himself, was thinking of doing the same thing, more so now than ever.

"So, you're okay with staying in?" Jeff asked him, his conversation with Maddie from the night before rolling through his brain.

"Honestly, no. That's the last thing I want to do, but you are the only family I've got. Where you go, I go." Derek had been raised as an orphan, choosing the join the military the day he turned eighteen so that he could get out of the group home he'd been placed in until he finished high school. He'd taken his GED and signed up.

He and Jeff had met during basic training and become best friends, following in each other's footsteps and pushing one another to do better each step of the way. Jeff met his friend's eyes. "I haven't made any decisions, but I'm with you. I don't think I can go back into the field, and the thought of training newbies for the next twenty years sounds like self-inflicted torture."

"So, what else is there?" Derek asked him as they picked up the seat portion of one of the benches. They headed back inside the building.

"I don't have an answer to that, but Maddie's happy here. I really like the people and what I've seen of the town so far. If I can figure out a way to have a career here, I'm up for staying in Castle Peaks. Maybe I can figure out a way we can both make a living here."

Derek nodded. The relief on his face at hearing that Jeff didn't want to stay in the military, and that he was willing to share what came next with him, was plain to see. Jeff silently vowed to do whatever was necessary to make sure they could both get out and live normal lives.

"So, Maddie doesn't have a clue about what's happening on Saturday?" Derek asked as they set the seat down in the solarium and headed back out to retrieve the base it sat upon.

"Not yet. Everyone is in on the surprise. Now we just have to try and keep everyone hidden until then."

"Hey, we're trained to stay undetected. Show us where we'll be staying and you won't see us until it's too late."

Jeff laughed at his friend. "You all have deluxe accommodations at a house on the outside of town. The owner wanted to show his appreciation for your service and he even hired a housekeeper/cook to be there for the remainder of the week."

"No joke? That's awesome," Derek told him, sharing the news with the other four men who echoed his enthusiasm.

"Let's finish carrying this stuff inside and you can follow me over there. I'll make sure you guys have what you need and then I need to head home for dinner. Maddie texted me a little bit ago and is making a special dinner for us tonight."

"Any special reason?' Austin asked with a waggle of his eyebrows.

Jeff shook his head and laughed. "Not really. Coming here has been a little nerve-wracking at times. We were only married for a few days before I had to fly out…it was kind of like coming home to a stranger, and yet not."

"But things are better?" Ian asked. He'd been married when he first joined the team, but his wife had left him after their first extended mission. She'd gone back to Texas, saying she couldn't stand worrying about him day and night. Ian had been devastated, and he continually kept tabs on her. It seemed she had been as heartbroken to leave him as he'd been to get her "Dear John" letter.

Jeff looked at him and nodded. "They are. How's Amelia?"

Ian's expression soured. "Pretty much the same. She won't take my phone calls, but my brother assures me she's still in love with me and won't give anyone else the time of day. I'm going home and I'm going to win her back. Even if I have to grovel."

"If you love her, don't give up. Once she realizes you're not going to leave again, hopefully she'll give you a chance."

"I think she will. I still love her and I think she still loves me, but she's scared. Now that I'm not going to be heading to some nameless country where people want to kill me, there's no reason for her to be scared any longer. I'll send you an invite to the wedding when we renew our vows."

"You do that and I'll be there."

"Me, too," Derek told him. "Okay, that's the last piece. Let's get out of here and see what our personal cook has planned for dinner."

Jeff laughed and then escorted the men out of the building with a promise to his helpers to return first thing in the morning. The solarium was almost finished and he was feeling very good about how this surprise wedding was coming together. Just a few more days and he'd get to enjoy the fruits of his, and everyone else's, labor.

Chapter 20

March 9th, Thursday morning…

"Are you sure you're going to be fine for dinner? The cafeteria food isn't all that bad," Maddie reminded him as she finished getting ready for her double shift.

"I'm sure. I'll grab something at the diner or just some leftovers from last night. Don't worry about me at all," Jeff told her with a smile.

"It's not that I'm worrying, I just feel bad leaving you to fend for yourself all day long. I shouldn't have taken Alaina's shift."

"But you're helping out a friend and I understand that. Now, how about I drop you off at work and that way, you won't have to drive home when you're tired later tonight? I'll pick you up then."

"Really?" Maddie asked him with a soft smile. "That's really a nice offer and I will definitely take you up on it. The last time I worked a double shift, I was so tired, I seriously gave consideration to sleeping on that vinyl couch in the nurse's lounge."

"No need to do that. I'll even draw you a nice bubble bath when you get home tonight."

"Throw in a foot rub and I will be forever in your debt," she told him, kissing him on the cheek. She grabbed her purse and headed for the door. "Now, if I don't get a move on, I'm going to be late and I hate doing that to the girls who worked the night shift."

Jeff grabbed his car keys and followed her out of the apartment. He was thrilled that she was going to be working a double shift. He'd be taking full advantage of the fact that she was stuck at the clinic with no way to get back into town, because she didn't have a vehicle. If something with her work schedule happened to change, he'd be the second to know about it. She being the first.

"So, the second shift ends at 11 o'clock. I should be ready to go by five after," Maddie told him as he pulled into the clinic's parking lot ten minutes later. The sun was shining and the weather was starting to warm up. Spring was definitely in the air and the weather report for this weekend was sunny skies and high 50's. A perfect forecast for a renewal of wedding vows.

"I'll see you tonight," Jeff told her, pulling her to him for a kiss before she could escape the vehicle.

"Bye," Maddie told him, shutting the door before heading towards the clinic doors. Jeff waited until she turned and waved at him as she entered the building, then he put the vehicle back in gear and drove off.

Today was full of last minute details. Maddie's parents would be arriving sometime around 6 o'clock this evening and Alaina would drive them straight to the Mercer residence. Cora had been asking him questions about their food likes and dislikes throughout the solarium project, and he had no qualms about leaving them in the capable housekeeper's hands. He hadn't had many answers for her, but then again, he'd never actually met Maddie's parents. He planned to correct that tonight.

His own parents would be arriving sometime tomorrow, as would the flowers and a variety of other items the women organizing most of the wedding had deemed necessary. Jane had arrived in town on Monday with her husband and Dr. Mike, and she was already working on the food that would be served at the reception after the ceremony.

The entire town of Castle Peaks had been invited, including a large number of outsiders. He had left the guest list up to Sara, knowing that she would probably know better than he did who Maddie would like to see.

His own guest list had included his parents and his teammates. They had been keeping a low profile at the Showalter house since their arrival Tuesday afternoon, but today they would be coming to town to try on tuxedos. In keeping with the ruse of a fundraiser and fashion show theme, his teammates were going to be the handsome escorts who assisted Maddie's bridesmaids down the aisle. Of course, Maddie would recognize several of them so they would be keeping a low profile until after she saw her father standing at the back of the chapel, ready to escort her down the aisle.

Ezra had insisted on being included and had assured Jeff that walking a hundred feet with only one crutch wasn't going to kill him. Jeff had ordered him to use both crutches and Derek had assured his best friend he would make sure Ezra obeyed. Jeff wanted everything to be perfect Saturday, and having to pick one of his teammates up off the floor wasn't even on the agenda. No, things were going to work like a finely tuned machine. Jeff could feel it in his bones.

*****

Later that evening...

"That was Alaina. She's coming up the driveway now," Jeff told Bill Mercer as the two of them sat in his den waiting for Maddie's parents to arrive.

"You look nervous, son," Bill commented with a chuckle.

"Well, sir. You had a daughter...If you found yourself in a similar situation as Maddie's dad, how would you react?"

Bill nodded his head and pursed his lips for a moment and then smiled. "I'd welcome him into the family, right after I made sure he realized the error of his ways."

Jeff blew out a breath, "That's what I was afraid you'd say. I spoke to her mom, but I haven't even had a phone conversation with her dad. What if he's against this marriage? I think that would break Maddie's heart. She loves her parents."

"She loves you and that will trump any protest they could possibly make. If they love her, they will respect her choices and not make her choose."

"I hope you're right, sir," Jeff told him, hearing Cora answering the front door and welcoming the people on the other side. "Here goes nothing."

Bill slapped him on the shoulder, "It will all work out just fine. Chin up."

"Yes, sir," Jeff told him, standing up straight and pulling his military training to the forefront. *No matter what happens in the next ten minutes or so, I will be strong and not give Maddie's parents any reason to think less of me. I can do this because it matters to her.*

He followed Bill from the den and into the brightly lit foyer, quickly taking stock of the burly man with the graying beard and his petite wife who looked exhausted. "Mr. and Mrs. Grantham, welcome to Castle Peaks. I'm Jeff Young."

He stepped forward and extended his hand to Wesley Grantham, only somewhat relieved when the man shook it, clasping it tightly in a bruising grip. The man didn't speak, but his eyes were very telling.

"Mrs. Grantham," Jeff extracted his hand to offer her the same greeting. She pushed his hand away and stepped forward, leaning up on her tiptoes and hugging tight before kissing him briefly on the cheek.

"I thought we had the name situation fixed?" she told him with a smile as she stepped back.

Jeff nodded. "Sorry. Catherine, I hope your flight wasn't too tedious?"

"It was fine," Wesley commented, his voice a bit gruff.

Jeff nodded and then turned to Bill. "This is Bill Mercer and it is his home you'll be staying in for the duration of your visit. This is his housekeeper, Cora." Now that introductions were done, Jeff found himself somewhat at a loss for words.

Bill picked up on his dilemma and solved the situation with perfect ease. "Why don't you two come on into the den and relax for a bit while Cora puts together a light supper?"

Cora beamed at them. "I was thinking hot sandwiches and soup?"

Catherine smiled back. "That sounds lovely. Can I help you in any way?"

Cora shook her head. "No, you get off your feet and get to know this fine young man." She turned to Alaina. "Dear, would you like to stay for supper?"

Alaina smiled and backed towards the door, "No, I'll bring their luggage in and..."

"I'll get it," Jeff told her, his upbringing and code of how to act around women kicking in.

"Thanks. I really do need to get home and take care of a few chores. I work the early shift tomorrow and I'm beat." She turned to the Granthams. "It was really nice to meet you. Maddie is a wonderful girl and I'm really happy for her. Mr. Mercer, I'll see you around the clinic."

"Good night, Alaina. Thank you again."

"I'll be right back. Please join Bill and just relax."

"Join us when you're done, son," Bill told him, leading the way down the small hallway.

Jeff nodded and followed Alaina to her vehicle, unloading the suitcases and then giving her a smile. "Thanks again."

"No problem. They seem like really nice people. They really love their daughter and just want to see her happy." She seemed kind of sad when she said that, and Jeff wasn't quite sure what to make of that.

"I also just want to see her happy. That's why I'm doing all of this."

"Well, if this doesn't make her cry happy tears, I don't know what will. See you Saturday."

Jeff nodded and picked up the luggage, easily carrying it up to the house and setting it on the tiled floor just inside the foyer. He headed to the den and was pleased to see Wesley looking more relaxed than when he'd first arrived. He took a seat opposite them, feeling like a bug beneath a microscope when Wesley and Catherine both turned their attention his direction.

"So, Catherine tells me you met Maddie at the hospital. Something about stitches?"

Jeff nodded, "Yes, a new recruit got himself into trouble on the obstacle course and, in the process of helping him get untangled from the barbed wire, I ended up getting cut by it. Maddie was the nurse who treated me at the hospital. She's a very good nurse."

Catherine smiled at him, "She is a compassionate nurse. I worry that she gives too much of herself to her patients and that she opens herself up to heartbreak."

Jeff nodded. "I've seen that firsthand, but I don't think she can be any other way. She doesn't shy away from dealing with situations that are likely to go poorly; instead, she gives them the same care and consideration she gives the patients who are likely to make a full recovery.

"The day I arrived here, she'd just lost a little girl and I found her crying brokenly in the clinic chapel. She seemed to embrace the grief and then she was able to move forward and be supportive for the family and other co-workers who were saddened by the loss. She's got an amazing inner strength."

Wesley nodded. "She's always had great compassion for those hurting around her. She was the little girl who befriended the weak and unattractive kids at school. She defended them to the bullies and popular kids and treated them the same way she treated everyone else. She has such a love for life and positive thinking...there are times I miss having her around. It's hard to be down in the dumps when she's always looking at the bright side of things."

"Every cloud has a silver and gold lining," Catherine told him with a smile. "Maddie loves to make people smile."

Jeff nodded his head. "She's very good at it, too." He paused and then met their eyes. "I would just like to apologize again, in person, for how things have gone down. Everything happened very quickly and we only had a few days before I flew out with my team."

"My wife said you are Special Forces?" Wesley asked.

Jeff nodded. "Yes, sir."

Wesley leaned forward and gave him a hard stare, "How long will you be gone the next time you deploy? How dangerous are these missions?"

Jeff kind of expected these type of questions, he just wished he had some hard answers. "Right now, I have another two months on furlough and then I will have to decide to re-up my time, or get out. I've been offered a desk job and while that would be much safer, it's not what I signed on to do in the military."

"What are you saying, son? Are you in, or are you out? And if you're in, where does that leave my daughter? Waiting for the blue suits to stop by and give her their condolences on your untimely death?"

Catherine whispered her husband's name and touched his arm, trying to shush him, but he demanded an answer. Jeff met his stare and answered as honestly as he could, "The last thing I want to do is leave Maddie again. Frankly, my last mission was so bad I don't know if I can go back into the field. I don't have an answer for you right now, but Maddie and I have discussed the future and have agreed that we will make that decision when the time comes. Together.

"I love your daughter and her happiness is paramount in this decision. Whatever we decide, it will be what we feel is right for our family and the future. You should know that we are praying for guidance and would welcome your prayers in this matter as well."

Catherine nodded and he could see unshed tears in her eyes. "You shall have them. Oh, I can't wait to see her. I brought the veil and I just know she's going to make a beautiful bride."

Jeff swallowed back his own unshed tears and nodded. "She's going to be shocked and so happy when she sees you both here. Sir, Bill has offered to drive you over to Evansville tomorrow morning for a fitting on your tuxedo. Castle Peaks doesn't have their own shop, but Evansville isn't a very far drive and that's where the rest of the tuxes are coming from."

Cora appeared in the doorway. "Supper is ready. Would you like to eat in the dining room, or in here?"

"I think we'll go to the dining room. I hope you plan on joining us," Bill told his housekeeper with a smile.

"Of course. I'll start bringing everything in and setting it up."

Catherine stood up and followed her from the room. "I insist you let me help you. I'm not used to being waited upon and don't plan to start now."

Jeff stood up and waited for Wesley to do the same. Bill exited the room, leaving him alone with his new father-in-law, and he waited as the man appeared to have something to say to him. He wasn't wrong.

"Jeff, I can't say I'm happy about being kept in the dark for almost a year, but I do understand new love and the circumstances you found yourself in were less than ideal. I love my daughter and her happiness is my only concern right now. You have our support in this marriage, but I strongly urge you to look at every option available to you in regards to the future. Maddie may have survived your absence this time out of sheer will and stubbornness, but if she has to do so again, the outcome might not be the same."

"Sir, the last thing I want to do is leave your daughter again. She was the only thing that kept me going over there. It was bad. Think of all of the videos and reports of how jihadists' treat their prisoners and that wouldn't be far off. I lost four men over there and will live with that for the rest of my life. I know I couldn't do anything to save them, but they were under my watch. Maddie is also under my watch and I will not willingly put her in harm's way again. She stood by me and for that I am ever grateful. I understand what a blessing and a gift she is to my life, and I thank God daily that she didn't give up on me. I'm going to do everything in my power to see I don't take advantage of being given a second chance with her. I promise."

Wesley watched him for a minute and then nodded his head. "That's good enough for me. Welcome to the family, son."

Jeff found himself being hugged and he offered up a silent prayer of thanksgiving for how this first meeting had gone. This was the biggest hurdle to cross in his mind, and everything had gone better than he could have imagined. Now, he only had to keep everyone hidden until Saturday morning.

Chapter 21

March 11^{*th*}*, Saturday morning...*

Maddie walked into the clinic dressed in her favorite jeans and an old sweatshirt. She'd been told the day before to not worry about makeup or doing her hair, and after having woken up late, that was just fine with her. Today was a fundraiser for the clinic. The staff had been told the day before that there would be a variety of special guests with them, and that everyone was expected to attend.

Maddie was still slightly confused about how the fundraiser was supposed to work, but she'd heard there was to be a fashion show and a reception over at the church later. Jeff had insisted on driving her to the clinic this morning and told her that he'd be available to drive her over to the church later as well.

He planned to attend the fundraiser but said he needed to do a bit more work on the solarium first. Maddie hadn't had a chance to stop by the church and see the progress that was being made, so she looked forward to going to the reception to check things out for herself. She pushed through the doorway and was immediately grabbed by Alaina and Jess. "Hey! You're late!"

Maddie smiled. "Sorry, I kind of overslept. That double shift took a lot out of me."

"Well, there is no time to lose. We have an emergency and I'm hoping you're the right size."

"Right size for what?" Maddie asked as she was hustled into the smaller cafeteria where chaos seemed to be the order of the day.

Jess and Alaina didn't respond. Instead they dragged her over to a row of what appeared to be wedding dresses. "Here she is."

A smartly dressed man turned and clapped his hands upon seeing her, "Oh, she'll do nicely."

"Do nicely? For what?" Maddie asked as she was pulled over to a three-way mirror that was set up around a small platform.

"One of the photo shoots is a wedding scene, but all of the dresses are too long for Alaina and everyone else declined to play the bride. You're the only person left so one of these dresses had better fit."

"You want me to dress up like a bride? Guys, this probably isn't a very good idea. I didn't even wear a wedding dress when I married Jeff. Can't someone else…"

The man shook his head, "There is no one else. Now, step behind this screen and remove those…clothes."

Maddie raised an eyebrow at the man, but Jess didn't give her a chance to decline. She pulled her behind the screen and handed her a strapless bra. "I think that's your size."

Maddie looked at the bra, then at her former roommate. "Jess, this is a really bad idea…"

"No, it's perfect. They wanted me to be the bride, but none of the dresses fit. Not even close."

Alaina peeked around the screen, "I'm going to start bringing dresses in. Jess, will you help her try them on?"

"Sure. I hope this works, otherwise we're going to have to get the photographer to rethink their entire shoot."

Maddie didn't like the sound of that and gave both women a smile. "Okay, let's see what we can make work." She wasn't exactly warming to the idea, but the thought of playing dress-up had always appealed to her and she was willing to do what she could to help make the fundraiser a success.

They tried on dress after dress, but the sixth one seemed to be made for her. It was an ivory satin gown, with a sweetheart neckline, a lace inset on both sleeves, and a long train that would drape behind the person wearing the dress in an elegant display of beading and further lacework.

She turned and allowed Jess and Alaina to do up the numerous small buttons on the back of the gown. Then she was led around the screen to the gasps of those watching.

"Maddie! That gown looks like it was made for you," Sara told her, coming forward with a brilliant smile upon her face. In fact, the dress had been custom made from the picture of her mother's dress that Jeff had provided the dressmaker. It had been altered with a few temporary stitches to help cinch in the waistline. The man with the measuring tape draped around his neck wasted no time in getting her to step up on the platform and going to work on making the gown fit perfectly.

Maddie looked up at her reflection in the mirror and felt tears fill her eyes. *Gosh, this is almost like mom's dress. I could have never worn it, but...* She forced those "what if" thoughts out of her mind. She wasn't one given to regrets, and even though she'd not had the church wedding of her childhood dreams, she did have the man she believed was meant for her. That was what counted.

"Maddie, you look absolutely gorgeous." Alaina turned to the other staff members standing around and clapped her hands. "Okay, we have a bride. If you're dressing up as a bridesmaid, now would be a good time to do that. The photographer is over at the church setting up and wants to take some pictures at noon."

Alaina turned to her and smiled. "There are makeup and hair people here as well. The folks from the beauty salon over in Evansville even offered their services today so that everyone could look their very best."

Maddie stood still while the dressmaker continued to make a few final alterations to the gown she was wearing. "This seems like such a lot of trouble to go through for a fundraiser..."

Sara was standing to her left and shook her head. "Not when you think of all the good we do for people who otherwise couldn't afford to come here. Many of the treatments we offer here are considered experimental and therefore most insurance companies won't cover them. I hope one day that changes, but until then, I'll continue to seek generous donors to make up the difference."

Maddie's mind wandered back to Annsley and her parents. They were prime examples of a cancer patient whose insurance hadn't even come close to covering the cost of her treatments. Just like some of the other facilities scattered around the country, patients who came to the Mercer-Brownell clinic left without owing a dime to the facility. Maddie was pleased to have a small part in helping that blessing continue.

Fifteen minutes later, she was led over to a high stool where several people began working on various parts of her person. Her nails were painted a delicate pink color, her face was expertly made up and her red hair was straightened and then curled so that it fell in gentle curls about her face.

Maddie saw Grace wander into the room and waved to her. "Hey, are you feeling better?"

Grace gave her a smile and then pulled up a stool. "I am. Sara told me you were the one who recommended the hypnotist idea. Thank you. Mike talked to the guy in Denver and we're going down there on Tuesday to give it a try."

Maddie reached out and squeezed Grace's hand, "That's wonderful news. I know you're prepared for the worst, but I'm praying for a simple explanation and a healthy report."

Grace smiled at her. "Thank you. That means a lot."

Alaina and Jess appeared a few minutes later with several boxes of shoes in hand. They slipped them over her feet and gave Maddie the choice. She had never been that keen on high heels and she chose the small leather ballet flats with the beading on the tops.

"Those are perfect," Tori told her, coming forward with Emily and Daniella in tow. Sara's oldest daughter was following behind, and all three girls were dressed in frilly hot pink dresses with baskets hanging over their arms.

Maddie grinned at the girls. "Let me guess, you guys are the flower girls?"

Emily nodded her head. "Yes."

"I get to throw flowers at people." Daniella told her with a little hop in her step.

Grace turned and gave her daughter a shake of her head. "No, you get to throw flowers at the ground. Not at people."

Daniella made a face and then she brightened, "I can throw them up in the air first."

Maddie grinned, "Yes, you can throw them up in the air."

Grace looked at Maddie with fear on her face. "That might not be the best idea…"

Maddie laughed, "This is just for pretend. Let her have some fun. If the photographer can't deal with it, he shouldn't be in this line of work." She looked up and saw Alaina standing to the side, trying not to pay attention to the little girls, but there was a wistful look on her face Maddie couldn't explain. *I need to get to know her better. Something's not quite right with her. She seems so sad sometimes. Maybe next week we can go to lunch or something…She hasn't been here very long and she might just need a friend to talk to. I'm a very good listener.*

*****

Across town at the church, Jeff was beginning to get nervous. It was currently 11:30 and he's just heard from Sara that everything was moving along as planned. They would be leaving for the church in approximately ten minutes and he needed to make sure everyone and everything was in place when they arrived.

The guests had all been instructed to arrive no later than 11:30 and the sanctuary of the small chapel was currently filled to the brim. Maddie's mother had already been seated on the left side of the chapel, and his parents were seated on the right. The groomsmen were currently waiting in the wings and would begin escorting the bridesmaids down the aisle as they arrived.

Timing was everything in this little operation, and Jeff and Derek had joked that their years of training in the military had prepared them for this better than any hospitality course might have done.

"Okay, Sara just arrived and everything is set up in the solarium. The flowers are waiting for the bridesmaids, and the bride's bouquet is stunning," Derek told him with a grin.

Jeff grinned back. "I didn't know you were a connoisseur of flower arrangements. Have you missed your calling?" he teased.

Derek shook his head, "Not hardly. My sister owns a floral shop, remember?"

"Yeah, I remember." Jeff took a deep breath and then felt for the ring in his pocket. He'd rejected the idea of finding a ring bearer, instead choosing to keep the addition to Maddie's original wedding band on his own person. "Why am I so nervous?"

"Because this is important to you," Derek told him.

Sara came rushing from the direction of the solarium, "They're almost here. Is everyone ready?"

Derek nodded just as Trent pulled up with the first bridesmaids in the backseat. "Game time."

The groomsmen lined up, having been matched with the bridesmaids by height. Jess was acting as the matron of honor and would walk down the aisle on Derek's arm. Because of the need to keep things low key, none of the bridal party had met one another yet, and Jeff had just a moment of nerves as they women began their walk towards the chapel.

They were all smiling and laughing and he couldn't help but smile at the joy on their faces. Trent parked the car and entered after them, shaking Jeff's hand and suggesting he get in his position at the front of the altar. Jess was coming in the same vehicle with Maddie and they were pulling into the church parking lot right now.

Jeff nodded and then told him, "Thanks for making this possible."

"If the look on your girl's face is anything to go by, she's never going to forget this day."

That's what I'm hoping for. He headed for the side of the sanctuary and stopped to speak with Wesley one last time. "They're pulling up right now. Jess will come in first. The photographer is going to stop Maddie just outside the doors for a few pictures to give Jess enough time to get in place."

Wesley nodded and pulled on the vest of his tuxedo. "I'm supposed to wait until Jess goes in and then take up my place in front of the sanctuary doors."

"That's right. Cora will be waiting in the wings with a box of tissues, just in case they're needed."

Wesley nodded and then chuckled, "I might need one of them myself. This is a good thing you're doing here, son."

"Thanks." Jeff heard the outer door open and spied Jess walking in. "Oops! I need to get in position. See you at the front of the altar."

Jess saw him and waved him away. "She's coming! Hide!"

Jeff laughed. "I'm going right now." He made his way down the side hallway and slipped in the side door of the sanctuary just as the church pianist changed to the song before the wedding march. Jess entered on Derek's arm. Jeff felt his hands begin to sweat and he swung his glance over to his mom and dad. His mom was already crying, and his dad looked stoic.

He glanced away and caught Maddie's mom doing her best to control her own tears on the other side of the chapel. He took a quick breath as Derek reached his side and felt his best friend chuckle. He kept his eyes trained on the back of the chapel, but murmured loud enough for his friend to hear, "Your time is coming."

Derek murmured right back, "Not happening."

Jeff smirked and took a look around at all of the people present. There were several contenders in the single young woman department, and if he ended up staying and making Castle Peaks his and Maddie's home, he'd be helping Derek find someone to share his life with in short order. He'd never been happier than he was right now, and he wanted his best friend to experience that for himself.

Chapter 22

Maddie made her way out of the vehicle, smiling at Bryan as he handed her up onto the sidewalk. Jess handed her the train of her gown and helped her drape it over her arm with a grin, "Who knew these fancy dresses could be so difficult to move around in?"

Maddie nodded. "Maybe this is why most brides get dressed at the church?"

Jess nodded. "Probably." She headed up the sidewalk and then waved to the man with the camera around his neck. He stepped out onto the sidewalk and asked her to pose for him. When Maddie joined her, he took a few shots of them together, smiling and laughing as if they didn't have a care in the world.

"Ladies, these shots are wonderful. Maybe I could have a few of the bride by herself?" he asked, playing his part to perfection.

Maddie grinned. "Why of course, fine sir."

Jess laughed. "I'm going to get inside. See you in there."

The photographer waved her off, turning his full attention back to Maddie. "Okay, just act natural and smile for the camera. Remember, this is supposed to be the happiest day of your life so far."

Maddie grinned, "So far?"

He nodded and started snapping pictures. "I've heard this pales in comparison to the first moment you hold your son or daughter."

Maddie thought about that and then nodded. "I can see that. Do you have any kids?"

The photographer shook his head, looking over the top of the camera with a wink. "Not yet. My wife and I have only been married a few months. She teaches first grade over in Evansville and we wanted to enjoy being a couple for a while before we became mom and dad."

Maddie giggled. "Diapers and cranky infants can definitely put a damper on the couple thing."

"You talk like you have children." he told her, dropping his camera and coming to her side.

"Not yet, but I babysat all the time when I was in high school. I've changed more than my fair share of diapers and that was all before I turned nineteen." Maddie had been highly sought after by the young couples in their church and her neighborhood. Kids seemed to like her and it hadn't come as a surprise to anyone when she'd decided to focus her nursing skills on pediatric patients.

"Well, for today, you are a blushing bride. Let's get you inside and we'll take some more photos with your lovely ladies in pink." He held open the door and Maddie stepped inside, pausing for a moment to let her eyes adjust to the dimmer interior. The photographer moved ahead of her, fading into the background as Maddie walked towards the closed doors of the sanctuary. A man was standing with his back to her, as if waiting for the doors to open, and she walked up on his left, something about him seeming familiar.

She came up on his side and turned her head, intending to say something polite, but he turned his head at the same time and she gasped, tears filling her eyes. "Daddy?"

Wesley turned and looked at his beautiful daughter, tears making his eyes water. "Maddie! Oh, what a beautiful bride you are."

"Daddy!" Maddie's voice rose as she threw her arms around her father and hugged his neck. "What are you doing here?" she pushed away from him and then looked at his attire before looking around the foyer for her mother. "Where's mom?"

"She's already inside."

Maddie looked at the tuxedo he was wearing again. "Why are you dressed like that?"

"How else would you expect me to dress as I walk my daughter down the aisle?" he asked with a smirk.

"What? Dad, this is just a pretend photo shoot for a fundraiser..." She broke off as she started to realize how silly that sounded. Everything that happened this morning was beginning to make sense. "How? I don't understand...where's Jeff? Have you met Jeff?"

"How do you think your mother and I came to be here? Jeff called and explained everything. We flew in Thursday and a nice young woman, Alaina, picked us up in Boise and drove us here. Jeff feels horrible that he couldn't give you the wedding of your dreams and this is his way of correcting that error. His parents are waiting to meet you inside."

Cora stepped forward, a box of tissues in one hand and a beautiful bridal bouquet in the other. "They're ready for you now." She handed Maddie the bouquet and a tissue. "Dry your tears, dear. Brides should be happy on their wedding day." She then reached for a small table and produced a bridal veil Maddie had seem numerous times.

"Mom's veil?" she asked in a whisper.

"Yes. She wanted you to wear it."

Maddie nodded and bent her knees slightly as Cora attached it to her head. Her father kissed her on the forehead and then pulled the veil over her face. It was a half veil, barely reaching the bottom of her jawline, and a perfect match for the ivory satin of her dress. "Beautiful."

Maddie was completely overwhelmed. *Jeff did this? How?* She dried her tears and then handed Cora the tissue, "The flowers are beautiful."

"You can thank your colleagues for that and everything else today. The entire town helped pull this together for you and Jeff."

Maddie started crying again and her father wrapped an arm around her shoulders. "You're going to have everyone in tears if you don't stop. Let's go greet your husband. He's waiting at the front of the chapel for you."

Maddie nodded her head and took a steadying breath as Cora pulled the door open next to her. The music inside changed as her father opened the other door and everyone in the sanctuary surged to their feet. She looked straight ahead and saw Jeff waiting for her. He looked so handsome, dressed in a dark tuxedo. She glanced over the rest of the bridal party and recognized members of his team dressed alike. She saw her mother crying openly and reached over and hugged her as they reached the front of the sanctuary.

Pastor Jameson was smiling indulgently from the platform. Her father stopped with her in the front of the church and the pastor waved everyone to be seated. "Who gives this woman to be married to this man?"

Maddie looked at her father and heard him speak, "Her mother and I do." He then pushed the veil back and placed her hand in Jeff's waiting one.

Jeff gave her a watery smile and Maddie felt tears run down her cheeks. "I can't believe you did this."

"Are those happy tears?" he asked, searching her eyes for the answer.

Maddie nodded, handing her bouquet to Jess when she stepped forward to take it. "Thank you. All of you, thank you so much."

"You deserve to have the wedding of your dreams. I'm so sorry we didn't do this the first time around...I wanted to fix that."

"This does that," she told him with a waver in her voice and a small laugh. "This is amazing."

Jeff smiled down into her eyes and then asked, "Mrs. Young, would you do me the extreme honor of marrying me again? In front of all of these people?"

Maddie leaned up and kissed his cheek. "The honor is mine."

Pastor Jameson cleared his throat as the crowd murmured and giggled behind them, "I realize you've already said your vows once, but we typically leave kissing until the end of the ceremony."

The crowd's laughter rose and Maddie blushed as Jeff helped her climb the three steps to the top of the platform. "My apologies, pastor."

Pastor Jameson smiled at them both and then began the ceremony. The vows were traditional, and the entire ceremony only took about fifteen minutes before he was pronouncing them, again, husband and wife. Jeff looked down into her face and then tenderly kissed her lips. "Maddie, I love you."

"I love you, too."

Jeff turned them around to face the gathered crowd and then high fived Derek as he led Maddie down the steps. Her parents stepped forward and hugged them both and then it was his mom and dad's turn. "Maddie, may I introduce my parents, Faith and Scott Young."

Faith stepped forward and hugged Maddie, tears wetting both of their cheeks. "You are a beautiful bride and I can see how happy Jeff is. Congratulations."

Maddie nodded. "Thank you."

Jeff smiled and then Derek leaned forward and whispered something in his ear. Jeff looked at the back of the chapel and saw Trent and Sara waving him forward. He leaned down and whispered in Maddie's ear, "There still more to this day. Come on."

Maddie looked at him in shock "More?"

Jeff nodded and as they walked down the aisle, he was pleased to see that Annsley's parents had already removed themselves to the solarium. He smiled at Trent and Sara, leading Maddie down the hallway towards the rest of her surprise. Pastor Jameson had been instructed to let the bridal party leave the chapel before allowing the wedding guests an opportunity to join them.

He pushed open the doors of the solarium and led her inside. Christmas lights had been strung up around the perimeter of the structure, and a plethora of blooming plants and small trees created a virtual garden of paradise. Stone benches, gurgling fountains, and a continuation of the wedding decorations made sure Maddie knew this was all done for her and Jeff.

"It's spectacular!" she told him, turning around and then gathering up the train of her gown so it wouldn't get tangled in the plants. "You did all of this?"

Jeff smiled, "I had lots of help." He nodded up ahead, "There are some people here who would like to congratulate you."

Maddie turned and followed the pathway, finding Caroline and Clark Graves waiting for her with their other children by their side. "Oh! What are you doing here?"

Maddie hurried to meet them and exchanged hugs with them. Caroline gave her a kiss on the cheek and then handed her a small card. "Sara invited us here to see the solarium dedicated and to commemorate all of the children who have fought so hard to live."

Maddie felt tears fill her eyes, "Annsley…"

"…would have been thrilled to see you today. Do you remember what she asked you that last day?" Clark asked her.

Maddie swallowed and nodded, "I do. She wanted to know what I was waiting for."

Caroline smiled at her, "You didn't answer her then. Can I assume you aren't waiting any longer?"

Maddie felt Jeff come up and place an arm around her waist. She smiled up into his loving eyes. "No, I'm not waiting any longer."

Caroline and Clark shared a look and then Caroline nodded to the card Maddie had yet to look at. "When we were going through Annsley's things, we found a picture she'd drawn. Clark scanned it into his computer and has turned it into the logo for the foundation we've started in Annsley's memory. The money raised will go to help fight pediatric cancer."

Maddie gave her an encouraging smile. "Annsley would like that." The little girl had been full of positive energy and even though she'd been so sick, she'd always had a smile for others. She had definitely impacted the lives of those she'd met.

Maddie looked down at the card and smiled at the picture of a smiling Annsley on the front. She was wearing one of the brightly patterned skull caps the children favored when their natural hair all fell out after receiving chemotherapy. Her eyes were bright and Maddie realized she didn't even really notice the faint circles beneath her eyes or the way her skin was almost translucent and pale. She was still one of the most beautiful little girls Maddie had cared for.

"She looks so happy here," Maddie murmured, catching Caroline's eye and then making sure Jeff could see over her shoulder.

Maddie turned the card over and covered her mouth with one hand. A childish drawing of a small child dressed in what appeared to be a hospital gown was holding hands with what Maddie had to assume was a depiction of herself in a nurse's uniform. Her red curly hair and green eyes were hard to dismiss and the drawing had been enhanced and the words "Annsley's Hope" had been intertwined with the figures.

The drawing would have drawn an emotional response from Maddie, but it was the motto of the campaign that had tears running down her cheeks unchecked. "What are you waiting for?"

Jeff pulled her into his arms, offering her comfort and a shoulder to cry on. "Maddie told me about her last minutes with Annsley."

Clark seemed concerned. "We didn't want to ruin your wedding…"

Jeff shook his head, pulling her a little closer to his chest. "You didn't. Maddie's just overcome with emotion right now. I'm going to take her out of here for a minute and let her calm down. We'll be back for the dedication ceremony." He turned her and led her out the closest exit, taking her into a vacant room on the other side of the building from the chapel.

Maddie went with him, overwhelmed with everything that had happened thus far. "That drawing…I've never had a patient affect me so much."

"You and she had a special connection. You'll always carry a piece of her in your heart."

Maddie nodded, taking the tissues he found and trying to repair the damage her crying spell had created. "This is hopeless," she told him, wishing she had a mirror.

Jeff tipped her chin up and then took the tissue from her hands, wiping beneath her eyes and then kissing her on the nose, "You look beautiful. Never doubt that."

Maddie rested her head back on his shoulder, "I still can't believe you pulled this off."

"Believe it. We're going back to Georgia with your parents on Monday and then we'll go to Utah before coming back here."

Maddie lifted her head. "What about my job?"

"Sara thinks it's more important for you to spend time with me and our families. She approved you for a week of vacation and a week of personal leave. Your job will be here waiting for you when we return."

Maddie was quiet for a moment and then asked, "What about the future?"

Jeff sighed. "I wish I had an answer to that question. Derek and I talked and he doesn't want to resign either. He has no family...I am the closest thing he has and he's vowed to go wherever I do. I don't know what I could find to do around here, but I'm willing to look around."

Maddie smiled. "So, you're not going back in the field?"

"I'll have to formally resign and get discharged, but no...I have no interest in working for Uncle Sam any longer. You are my future and my responsibility now. I want to know that, when I wake up tomorrow, it's your face I'm going to see. I want to raise a family with you. I want to grow old with you."

Maddie searched his eyes, her heart bursting with love for this amazing man. Jeff had been somewhat romantic when they'd first met and gotten together, but what he'd managed to pull off today was over the top. He'd made all of her dreams come true and then some. She knew he'd had help from some of her co-workers and the townspeople. She was grateful and, now that Jeff was actually considering living in Castle Peaks permanently, she couldn't wait to see what their future held.

She looked down at the wedding ring he'd presented her with and watched the light bounce off of the diamonds. Annsley's words came back to her mind. "Your waiting is over."

As Jeff led her back into the solarium and the festivities continued, Maddie found herself cataloging everything so she could look back on this day and remember how happy she'd been. She knew there would be trials and tribulations ahead for her and Jeff, and possibly the town of Castle Peaks, but with love on their side...they would always survive and come out the winners. She was proof that patience and following your heart, no matter how impossible it might seem in the moment, always paid off in the end.

Epilogue

March 14th, Tuesday, Denver Jewish Hospital...

Grace sat in the small physician's office, holding her husband's hand, and wishing she were anyplace other than here. It was going on 5 o'clock in the evening, and they'd been at the hospital since around 9:30 that morning. She'd participated in a biopsy procedure where hypnosis was used instead of anesthesia.

She had easily succumbed to the hypnotist's charms and had been brought back to consciousness and hour later with only a slight ache in the biopsy site beneath her arm. They'd used a long needle to withdraw some of the tumor material, and it had been rushed to the laboratory for analysis.

Michael and she had decided to stay at the hospital and wait for the results, rather than heading home right away. It was now seven hours since the procedure had been carried out and the results were in. Grace took a shaky breath, letting it out slowly and recalling Maddie's words of encouragement. *I'm praying for a good report. So am I.*

Dr. Sekulow came into the office carrying a chart with him. He gave them both a friendly smile and then sat down behind the wooden desk. He looked at Grace and asked, "How are you feeling?'

"Nervous. Anxious. Only a little bit of pain."

"Well, keep taking those painkillers at least for the next few days." He tapped the chart he'd carried in with him. "Your biopsy results are back."

Grace nodded and Michael wrapped an arm around her shoulders, before addressing the physician. "Please, just give it to us straight. You don't have to sugarcoat anything."

Dr. Sekulow nodded and grinned. "Well, that's a relief. Especially since there's not much here to work with."

Grace was watching him and asked, "What are you talking about?"

"The tumor is completely benign."

"It's not cancerous?" Maddie asked in a whisper.

"No. It's not. In fact, the swollen lymph nodes will probably go down on their own."

Grace was so relieved and she threw herself into her husband's arms. Michael cradled her to him and then looked at the physician. "Thank you, doctor."

"You are very welcome. Now, there's one more piece of information I think I should share with you."

"Really? I'm afraid I can't imagine what that might be," Mike informed him.

"I don't imagine you can. Grace mentioned in our phone consult that she'd been experiencing nausea at all times of the day and night. Since we know it's not cancer, I asked our resident ob/gyn doc to do a welfare check on your unborn baby."

Grace nodded, so relieved to know that she didn't have cancer, she felt like jumping and screaming at the top of her lungs. She'd been so worried, and for nothing. *Thank, God!*

Mike was listening intently as the doctor described the ultrasound that had been performed on Grace while she was still hypnotized. Grace was only partially listening, but one word caught her attention and wouldn't be ignored. She lifted her head up and stared into the physician's eyes. "Did you just say, 'twins'?"

Mike reached for her hand and the physician nodded. "Yes. That's why there was an unusual heart rhythm. There are two babies, not one. Twins."

Grace looked at her husband and stood up, only to do the one thing she'd tried to avoid. She fainted into his outstretched arms.

*****

While Jeff and Maddie were off celebrating their second marriage and getting to know each other's families, things were getting back to normal in Castle Peaks for almost everyone. Everyone except Derek Evans. Derek was at loose ends and, when Jeff and Maddie had offered him the use of her apartment while they were gone, he'd jumped at the chance to stay in the small town for a bit longer.

He knew Jeff was leaning towards staying there on a more permanent basis, and after meeting the people Maddie worked with, he could understand why. These were good people who truly cared for one another. It was so much like the small town where he'd grown up, it was hard to imagine going back to Colorado Springs for more than enough time to pack up his meager belongings and get back on the road.

This morning he'd driven down to the diner, liking the camaraderie he felt amongst the other townsfolk who stopped by for a donut, a cup of coffee, or just to start the day with a good conversation.

"Have you decided what you're going to have?" Tamara asked. Derek knew she and her husband owned the diner and between them. They provided the only means of eating outside of cooking for oneself. Castle Peaks didn't have any fast food joints, and no restaurants other than the Peaks Diner. And Derek was fine with that.

"I have the two-egg special. Over easy with toast and coffee."

"Sure thing. You're a friend of Jeff's?" she asked as she scribbled his order down on her pad.

"I'm part of his team."

Tamara smiled at him. "Well, I know you boys probably don't hear it enough, but the people here thank you for your service to this country. Without you, this world would be a much different place to live in."

Derek nodded, always embarrassed when people showed their appreciation for a job he loved. Or...a job he had loved. After the last mission had gone awry, he wanted out. The only reason he would re-up would be Jeff, but he was fairly certain Jeff was getting out as well. That was good and now he just needed to figure out what to do with the rest of his life.

At the age of twenty-seven, he'd been in the military his entire adult life. He had no college education, but he could shoot a target at four hundred yards, wire an entire building to come down, and hike three miles with a fifty-pound pack on his back in under twenty minutes. He was the epitome of a lean, mean fighting machine, but he no longer had the desire to fight Uncle Sam's hidden wars.

A tinkling bell over the front door caused him to turn his head and watch as a petite little blonde came into the diner and stopped at the cashier. She spoke quietly to Tamara, who reached beneath the counter and produced a to-go box. She paid for it and turned to leave, catching Derek watching her and blushing before ducking her head and leaving the diner.

Derek was still staring after her when Tamara arrived with his meal a few moments later. "Who was that?"

Tamara followed his gaze out the window and then shook her head. "Alaina. One of the saddest women I've met in a long time. She's suffered some terrible loss or pain, but I haven't figured out what yet. She doesn't appear willing to let herself grieve and move forward and I get the impression she's stuck somewhere in between living in the past and living with the past."

"There's a difference," Derek stated as a fact, not a question.

"Yes. She needs someone, or something, to help her get out of the middle."

Derek ate his breakfast. He couldn't seem to get the young woman out of his head. She was a pretty little thing, maybe only coming up to his shoulder in height, and her blonde hair had just a hint of strawberry in it. He couldn't tell, but he thought her eyes were a blue-grey color. He'd seen her at the wedding, but it was obvious she'd been helping keep everything running smoothly and he'd not had a chance to talk to her.

As he finished his breakfast and tossed some bills on the table top, he decided he was going to make Alain his special project. Derek had grown up with an older sister and knew the value to be found in having someone to pour out your troubles to. Alaina looked like someone who desperately needed an ear to listen. There was something about her that drew his attention, and she'd intrigued him. He had to find out more about her.

He headed down the sidewalk, the local hardware and feed store his destination. If there was any useful gossip about the young beauty to be had, good or otherwise, the hardware store was the best place to hear it. While the women might visit the beauty salon or the grocery store, men talked about other people over wrenches, horse equipment, and feed. That's just the way the world seemed to work. Derek loved a good mystery and intended to spend some time figuring out what the young beauty was trying to keep to herself.

Derek was an expert when it came to gathering intel on a person. He could find just about anything out with a computer and enough time, but he decided he was going to do this the old-fashioned way. He was going to get to know the target on a personal level. Starting now.

Thank You

Dear Reader,

Thank you for choosing to read my books out of the thousands that merit reading. I recognize that reading takes time and quietness, so I am grateful that you have designed your lives to allow for this enriching endeavor, whatever the book's title and subject.

Now more than ever before, Amazon reviews and Social Media play vital role in helping individuals make their reading choices. If any of my books have moved you, inspired you, or educated you, please share your reactions with others by posting an Amazon review as well as via email, Facebook, Twitter, Goodreads, --or even old-fashioned face-to-face conversation! And when you receive my announcement of my new book, please pass it along. Thank you.

For updates about New Releases, as well as exclusive promotions, visit my website and sign up for the VIP mailing list. Click here to get started: www.morrisfenrisbooks.com

I invite you to connect with me through Social Media:

- Facebook : https://www.facebook.com/AuthorMorrisFenris/
- Twitter: https://twitter.com/morris_fenris
- Pinterest: https://www.pinterest.com/AuthorMorris/
- https://www.instagram.com/authormorrisfenris/

For my portfolio of books on Amazon, please visit my Author Page:

Amazon USA: amazon.com/author/morrisfenris

Amazon UK:

https://www.amazon.co.uk/Morris%20Fenris/e/B00FXLWKRC

You can also contact me by email:

authormorrisfenris@gmail.com

With profound gratitude, and with hope for your continued reading pleasure,

Morris Fenris

Author of 'Second Chances Series'

Hey Willis Dyer
an repeating again
Lily name is taken off
the list of the documents
but keep it private we are
dealing with maturity
Willis Dyer we got
everything secured in UK now

Willis Dyer
you having nothing to loose.
but make sure you ~~dont~~ treat Lily
how it used to be
Very soon we all gonna jubilate
Willis Dyer dont get through ~~me~~
Sell any land

Hi Willis Dyer
Be careful and dont ~~sell~~ any land
Dont get disappointed by Lilly friends
or who even is trying to pretend
Willis dyer your a man of your words

Printed in Great Britain
by Amazon